DEDICATION

Many thanks to my brother, Andrew—had it not been for exposing me to Oi, punk, and other hardcore music in the 1980s, driving me around to record stores, and letting me borrow your records, I might never have discovered the music that is at the heart of this story.

Thanks are also due to all the punks, skins, and hardcores I've had the pleasure of meeting and befriending in my life. I got into this music when I was sixteen, and the connection I feel to it has never waned.

Thank you to all the students who continue to inspire me. No matter who you are, what you are, or what you choose to be, you remind me constantly that the journey is the reward.

And lastly, thank you to Shawn. There is no better friend, nobody who makes me want to be better than I am, than you.

Chapter 1

DRAGGING

The sun was too bright. The weather too hot. Tyler Ruiz wanted to be doing anything other than going to sixth period PE.

But I have to, he told himself.

Tyler was a sophomore at Banks High School. He hadn't been there very long, so blowing off PE wasn't an option. He had made the football team, and he wanted to stick with it.

Tyler had been kicked out of a few schools. It was always for fighting. He was a decent student until everything changed in middle school.

Tyler's mom died of cancer when he was twelve. He stayed with his grandmother until his dad returned from Afghanistan. His father was discharged with post-traumatic stress disorder.

Tyler would have gone back to live with his grandma. That's what he wanted to do. She was nice to him, unlike his father.

But his grandmother died when Tyler started ninth grade.

By the end of that spring, Tyler had almost made it through his freshman year at Miller High School. Then his teacher Mr. Green made fun of him. He called Tyler out about his clothes. He said they looked like "something you'd find at Goodwill."

Tyler lost it.

He attacked Mr. Green and found himself expelled. His dad really let him have it. He even kicked him out of the apartment for a week.

Tyler was tired. He was tired of school. Tired of his dad. Tired of his life.

But this wasn't why he felt off today. It had to do with the night before. What happened gave Tyler a completely new set of problems.

"And I didn't think my life could suck any more than it already does," he said aloud to no one in particular.

LATE-NIGHT LOSER

Adam Fields, the quarterback for the school football team, threw a party the night before. It was a team-only blowout.

Tyler got along well with everybody. So far. He hadn't made any lifelong friends, but everybody seemed to like him okay.

Adam lived in a big house. It was in Jake Gardens, which was the wealthiest section of town. It was also where Banks High School was located.

Tyler lived in the Via Joaquin apartments. They seemed like a million miles away from Banks. The Via Joaquin was low-income housing. Tyler shared a one-bedroom with his dad. He slept on the couch.

Compared to Jake Gardens, Via Joaquin was a slum.

The cheerleaders were also at Adam's party. Every one of them was perfect and gorgeous.

Tyler wasn't there five minutes when he started talking to Cassie Ramirez, Adam's girlfriend. She was tall, with dark skin and long black hair. She laughed at everything Tyler said.

"Want me to show you around?" she asked. "I'll get you a beer."

"Sure." Tyler smiled. He'd been told by many girls that he had a nice smile.

Cassie knew how to act at parties. Tyler figured she'd been to a lot. Cassie was a senior, after all.

"This house is huge." Tyler couldn't believe anybody could live in such a big home. That anybody could have this much space.

They continued walking, talking, and laughing.

Before Tyler knew what was happening, they were making out. He didn't mind. He was an attractive guy. Girls always threw themselves at him. Maybe not in a big house. Maybe not with a rich girl like Cassie, but Tyler was no stranger to hot girls.

She took his hand, and they walked around some more. Cassie even showed him Adam's bedroom. It was as big as the apartment Tyler shared with his dad.

"Hi, Rachel," Cassie said to a girl who appeared in the bedroom doorway.

Tyler looked at Rachel. She was tall, with thick red hair that looked great with the tight green dress she wore. Maybe he could hook up with her later on that night.

"Cassie." Rachel had a serious look on her face. "Adam's looking for you guys."

Rachel took Cassie by the arm. In seconds, they were gone. Cassie giggled as they left Tyler alone in Adam's big bedroom.

Normally, Tyler wouldn't have cared if Cassie had a boyfriend. He would've done anything with her.

"I don't know the guy," he'd said in the past. "If she wants to hook up with me, we'll hook up. If the couple has problems, that's on them."

Tyler knew he couldn't be like that now. He was too new at Banks High School. He couldn't start causing trouble. His dad would probably kill him. He said and did so many crazy things because of his PTSD.

He yelled about the war. About what happened to other guys in his unit. About men violently dying right in front of him.

He got physical with Tyler all the time.

Tyler wanted to help his dad. But it seemed like whenever he tried, this only made his father angrier.

Feeling a little out of place, Tyler left the party.

Chapter 3

Punk Chick

Tyler caught a ride to the party with one of the guys on the team. Since he left without telling anybody, he had to walk home.

Eight miles.

Tyler got home around one in the morning. Even though he was tired, he didn't go to sleep right away. It was hard to relax in his dad's apartment. He never knew when his father might go off on him. He couldn't count how many times he'd been jostled from sleep. Tyler couldn't remember the last time he'd slept through the night.

He was almost to the locker room. Banks High School was bigger than any school Tyler had ever attended. Sometimes he felt like he was being swallowed up.

Then he saw Sara Allen.

She had short black hair, bangs, and multiple piercings. Sara wore a tight T-shirt with the band Black Flag written across it. She had on brown skinny jeans and black Chuck Taylors.

Usually, Tyler wouldn't have given a girl like her a second look.

But he couldn't stop staring. He even slowed his pace. Sara had a confident walk. With her backpack worn over both shoulders, she seemed like she didn't care what anybody thought of her.

Tyler acted like that. But deep down he always felt like people were judging him. He figured that was why he got in so many fights.

"Look at me," he said to Sara under his breath. Tyler felt his heart beating faster. He desperately wanted to make eye contact with her. He wanted to have some kind of connection.

Sara kept walking. Then Tyler noticed she was smiling. She *had* noticed him.

For the rest of the day, Tyler found it almost impossible to think about anything but Sara's smile.

StEP ONE

By the way everybody was ignoring him, Tyler knew he was in the doghouse. He figured that word had spread about what had happened with Cassie. He knew it was only a matter of time before he would have to talk with Adam about it.

During summer practice Tyler hadn't been assigned a position. He was new to the team, and Coach Wagner wasn't sure where to put him.

Tyler was about five eleven with a muscular build. He kept his hair short because it was easier. He didn't have a job, so he couldn't afford things like hairspray. He figured with his size, the coach would find a spot for him eventually.

Today Coach Wagner stuck Tyler on the line. After running a play, he was tackled with a late hit by German Utria.

They landed hard, and German was quick to get off him. It didn't hurt, but it made Tyler mad.

"What the hell?" Tyler yelled.

"Just running the play, dude!" German yelled. He was about six two and even more physically imposing than Tyler.

"The play was over!" Tyler knew it was a mistake to push German after he said that. He couldn't help it.

Suddenly, Adam stepped in. He was about Tyler's size and build. Since he was the quarterback, he was the de facto team leader.

Only then did Tyler notice Cassie and the other cheerleaders practicing a cheer. They seemed to be watching the guys. Tyler figured she was smiling.

"Listen," Tyler started, "if you told him to take a late hit on me, there is no reason to do that."

"Really?" Adam smiled. He was getting the exact reaction from Tyler that he wanted.

"It's not my fault you can't handle your girl," Tyler stated. "Talk to her, not me."

"Please," Adam drawled. "Cassie would never take you seriously."

"Why not?" Tyler moved toward Adam. Again, he didn't want to, but he was so used to using his fists to solve his problems.

"Look, Tyler ..." Adam continued to have an ugly

smirk on his face. The one that told Tyler he was a loser. That Adam thought he was better than him. "It's not your fault your parents have no money. But from what I hear it *is* your fault you got sent to a school where no one wants you. You got kicked out of the last one, right, welfare boy?"

Everything went black for Tyler Ruiz. Just like so many times before.

Chapter 5

OLD HABITS

In a split second, Tyler's right fist crashed into Adam's face. Before his body hit the ground, Tyler managed to grab him. He hit Adam again. Blood poured from Adam's nose.

Images passed through Tyler's head as he jumped on Adam.

His dad yelling at him, slapping him on the side of his head.

The poor, dirty apartment that was the only place they could afford to live.

Mr. Green from his last school. Smiling as he insulted Tyler about his clothes. Smiling before Tyler belted him too.

Tyler was quick. None of the other football players had time to react.

As he landed numerous punches to Adam's face, Tyler

started to think about how bad he wanted to mess it up. Adam may have gotten all the breaks in life, but his looks were one thing Tyler could try to take away from him.

More blood gushed from the quarterback's nose and mouth as Tyler kept punching.

Chapter 6

BOUNCED

The other players finally pulled Tyler off Adam. He immediately tried to go after Adam again. It took the team's combined strength to keep him off. They moved him a few feet away. Now he was in front of Coach Galloway, the football team's head coach.

Coach Galloway was African American. He wasn't tall, but he had a way of talking that commanded respect. Tyler hadn't interacted much with Coach.

"Tyler." Coach Galloway's tone was stern. "You need to calm down, son."

The images of everything Tyler hated flashed through his mind. He just wanted to go to high school. To have the experience that everybody else seemed to take for granted. Nobody would let him. They wouldn't leave him alone.

Before Tyler could defend himself, Coach Galloway was in his face.

"Are you stupid? Do you think you can disrupt my practice by fighting?"

His teammates were still holding Tyler back. He stared stupidly at the coach. He couldn't think of a smart retort.

"You're gone," Coach Galloway finally said.

Tyler tried to break loose. He didn't know what he was going to do. He just had to be free. He didn't like anybody—except girls—putting their hands on him.

And then, like so many times before, campus security showed up. The football players holding him let go.

Tyler wanted to continue fighting, but he knew he couldn't. As campus security walked him off the field, Tyler knew he had blown it.

Any chance of things being different at Banks High School was gone.

Chapter 7

Principal's Office

Tyler sat in his sweat-soaked practice uniform across from Principal Cohen. He kept looking at the photos the man had on his desk and walls. They were of him with his family. From what Tyler could tell, he and his wife had a little boy.

His kid's life is already better than mine, Tyler thought. *In a few years I'll be eighteen, and my life will be over.*

"I really thought you wanted to do something here, Tyler."

One of the campus security guards made a noise. Principal Cohen had kept a guard in his office in case Tyler got physical again.

Tyler didn't think he was tough or hard. Other people had made him that way. He didn't even really want to play football. He only did it because he could. He wanted to be a part of something.

Tyler liked to write. He wrote a lot in elementary school. These days he mostly wrote only for school assignments, but sometimes he still did it just for fun. He had started a new story recently.

"Do you have anything you want to say?" Principal Cohen leaned a little closer. He was trying to reach Tyler.

This really burned Tyler up. He didn't want to be removed from people. They pushed him away. They ignored him. The only time people seemed to notice him was when he did something bad.

He shook his head. Nothing he was going to say would make this situation any better. Adam had started it, but people like him never got in trouble. Tyler may not have been smart to fight with Adam, but he knew enough to keep his mouth shut.

"I'm going to be placing you in OCS for three days. You'll have all your assignments brought to you. If you focus and stick to your work, you'll have all the time you need to complete everything."

OCS: on-campus suspension.

Tyler had been suspended so many times. At so many other schools. The school staff knew he would know what it meant.

Chapter 8

Dad

Tyler always made it a point to walk quickly through the halls of Via Joaquin. The small one-bedroom unit was located in a large multi-apartment building. The two-bedroom apartments were for larger families. You took what you were offered with Section 8 housing.

Tyler and his dad had only lived there for a few months. Tyler would nod his head in acknowledgment to other residents he passed every day. Some even knew his name. Many tenants seemed to have mental disorders. Others had physical disabilities. Caseworkers and therapists always seemed to be coming or going.

An older lady used to come and clean the Ruiz apartment. She would cook for them too. Tyler was not usually home when she was there. But he liked knowing she was coming. Tyler loved the food she made (tacos, his favorite). It was also nice to have another person around for his dad.

One day Tyler's dad got mad and threw some dishes at her. The woman never came back. Nobody ever came back.

Despite how his dad treated him, Tyler still loved him. It was mostly because somewhere inside his tortured father, Tyler believed that he still loved his son too.

Tyler dropped his backpack on the floor. He saw by how the mail was placed on the table that his father had gone through it. His dad didn't work, so all the money he got came from the government. Tyler had tried to get a job several times, but nobody would hire him.

He wished he could work. He wanted to help.

Tyler's dad moved through the room. He limped as he walked.

His father's leg had taken a lot of shrapnel when his Humvee was ambushed in Afghanistan. The muscles were permanently damaged.

His dad was wearing sweats and a long-sleeve T-shirt. He still kept his hair short, like it had been in the military. Tyler looked a lot like him.

His father went to the fridge and got himself a beer.

Tyler heard the beer bottle open.

Then the voice inside his head told him to duck.

He did.

The beer bottle flew threw the air and crashed into the wall, where it shattered. Glass and beer went everywhere.

Tyler glared at his father.

"You think you can just do whatever you want?" His father never started a conversation with a statement. It was always an interrogation.

He hadn't always been like this. Tyler remembered when he was fun. He used to pick Tyler up from school and take him to the beach. Or to the movies. Some weekends they'd go camping.

That was when his mom was alive. When they were "normal."

"You got suspended! It's only the first week!" His dad was yelling now. There had been complaints about him from other tenants. The few times he did go out, people stayed away from him.

"It's on campus, Dad. Don't worry. I won't be home." Tyler eyed his dad for a moment and looked away.

His dad moved close to him. Too close. Tyler would have punched anyone else for getting so close. But not his father.

"Don't mess up at this school." His dad's tone was low. And scary. "I can throw you out on the street any time I want. I'll go live somewhere else, and I won't even tell you where it is. You understand?"

"Yes." Tyler was sixteen. If he was on the street, who

knew what would happen to him? As much he hated Via Joaquin, he knew things could be much worse.

"Clean up that mess. Then get me another beer." His dad walked into the bedroom.

Tyler went over and grabbed some paper towels. As he cleaned up the beer and broken glass, he told himself not to think too much about what had just happened.

It's not gonna do you any good.

With his mind blank, somehow the face of that punk chick, Sara, came to him.

Tyler knew her image wouldn't last long, but it was great while it did.

From the bedroom Tyler heard his father's voice. He was yelling for his beer.

OCS

On-campus suspension was located in a small room that didn't have a window. It had no books either. Just five small desks. Facing those desks was a large desk with nothing on it. The walls were bare.

OCS was run by one of the campus security guards. He wore a dark blue and white tracksuit. He was an African American man named Leon. He was muscular, bald, and intimidating as hell.

Tyler sat at one of the desks. He was furious. He had nothing to do. Since first period was starting, he had no assignments yet. He didn't even have a phone he could look at. He couldn't afford to replace the one he'd shattered.

Not like he had many people to text. Tyler had friends at his old elementary school. But once his dad came home from Afghanistan, they started moving around. Tyler became a loner. The kind of kids he met didn't have families who tried to stay in touch.

Sara Allen walked into the room. At first Tyler thought maybe she worked in the office this period. He figured she was dropping something off. She had a white piece of paper in her hand.

Again, she wore a tight-fitting T-shirt that had the band the Business written across it. She had on black skinny jeans and combat boots. She was carrying a backpack that had patches for the bands 7 Seconds, the Civilians, and singer Tom Waits.

Sara skipped the desk next to Tyler. She seemed to want space between them.

"You're assignments from your classes should be coming any minute now." Leon eyed the attendance sheet. "Sara Allen."

Sara nodded her head as she put in her earbuds and took out her iPhone.

"Tyler Ruiz." Tyler nodded his head. "I don't mind if you guys want to talk or use your technology, but you better watch your language," Leon said. "And no taking pictures of people without them knowing and posting them. That happened once. Those students started fighting and found themselves expelled."

Leon eyed Sara and Tyler.

"I don't see that being a problem here," Leon muttered. Sara looked at Tyler for a moment and then looked away. He smiled slightly. A jolt of electricity went through his body.

Not Getting to Know You

Tyler finished his assignments in an hour. The work was easy. He figured that his teachers, counselors, and the principal thought he was dumb. Since he had a reputation for being violent, they were probably trying to get him through high school with the least amount of fuss possible.

The only class that had been difficult was English. Tyler liked to read and write. So he didn't mind the challenge.

He kept stealing glances at Sara. She didn't do any of her work. She just listened to music on her phone and texted.

The gears started to turn in Tyler's head. They were the only students there. He had all day—maybe more if Sara came back tomorrow and the next day. All Tyler had to do was get her to talk to him. Maybe he could turn this OCS thing into a hook-up.

Even as Tyler thought this, it didn't feel right. Even if they did get together, it wouldn't be enough for him.

He waved his hand at her. She didn't notice. This surprised Tyler and threw off his game. He waved again.

Sara looked at him dead-on. It was so quick and sent such a surge of electricity through him that his mouth hung open. He couldn't say anything. Sara made an irritated face and looked away.

"What're you listening to?" he finally asked.

"You wouldn't like it." Sara didn't meet his gaze again.

"How would you know what I like?" Tyler hoped he didn't sound too mad. He never let people get to him, especially girls.

"You're a jock. This isn't LMFAO crap."

"I don't even listen to LMFAO."

Sara made a face and eyed Leon, who was enjoying their conversation.

"Can you have him stop talking to me?" Sara's tone was emotionless.

"Leave her alone," Leon said with a smile.

"I don't want to talk to you anyway," Tyler stated.

"So why are you still talking?" Sara's voice got louder.

"At least the music I listen to isn't about loving Hitler. Racist!" Tyler had never been rejected like this in his life.

Sara laughed and rolled her eyes. She didn't look at Tyler.

He stared at her, seething. Tyler also couldn't help noticing that despite this bad beginning, he had gotten Sara to laugh.

CONNECTING?

There was one hour left in OCS.

Tyler had started writing a short story. He was stuck. It started off being about a superhero, but then it became about a firefighter rescuing a family. He made a mental note for tomorrow. *Bring my new story so I can work on it here.*

He was still stealing glances at Sara. After their "talk" she had pretty much sat at her desk, zoning out. Sara stared at the wall with an expression of amazement on her face. Almost like what was happening inside her head was incredible.

"I like Black Flag," Tyler offered. He couldn't explain it, but he hated that Sara thought she knew what he was. Maybe she did.

"Hey!" He eyed Leon after he said that. The last thing Tyler needed was to get in trouble for trying to hit on a girl.

"How do you know I like Black Flag?" Sara still wasn't looking at him.

"I saw you wearing their T-shirt yesterday."

"You did?"

"You knew I was looking at you. It was right before sixth period."

"I don't have a sixth period."

Sara looked at him now. This made Tyler feel better.

"You like Minor Threat?" he asked.

"Just because you know a few punk bands doesn't make you a punker." Sara made sure her words stung before she spoke again. "You're a jock."

"Jocks can't be into punk? That's like saying you can't be a punk because you go to school."

"I'm not a punker." Sara smiled slightly. "I'm a skinhead."

Tyler wanted to tell her that she had a pretty smile. He knew he couldn't. She'd just stop talking to him again.

"What's the difference? Punk or skin?"

"Skinheads stand for something. Anybody who knows anything about skins knows there are nonracist ones. The group started in England in the 1960s. The music skinheads like originally came from Jamaica."

"I was joking when I called you a racist." He smiled at Sara. "You made fun of me first."

"Stop talking to me." She looked away again. "I don't even know you."

"Fine, but I'm not what you think I am."

"I don't care what you are. I just want you to shut up."

Tyler couldn't explain it, but he liked Sara a whole lot more now. She was tough. She said what was on her mind.

He wasn't going to give up hope that he might have a shot with her. Tyler just needed to figure out a way in. Sara made him think, and that was a lot more than most other girls had asked of him.

SLIGHTLY STALKING

On-campus suspension was done for the day.

Sara couldn't have packed up her things and bailed any quicker.

Tyler watched her go. He wanted to follow her. He had to talk to her again.

Normally, Tyler would've let a girl like Sara go. He didn't believe in working too hard to win a lady's affections.

"There's always another one," he'd say.

But he couldn't stop thinking about her smile. The way she had confidently looked away from him the first time he saw her. Tyler didn't care what she said then. She had seen him look at her. Even if she hadn't looked back.

Tyler decided not to follow her. It had been a long,

boring day in OCS. Nothing about their conversations led him to think he'd get any different reaction outside school.

As Tyler walked out of school, he saw the football team practicing.

At that moment, Adam threw a long spiral. The receiver caught it. It was perfect. Effortless. If this were a real game, it would have been a touchdown.

I have nothing, Tyler thought. *Adam's life is just as good as it always was.*

He decided to head home before he got any angrier.

LIFE WITHOUT A DAD

Tyler flipped through the mail. Aside from his father's disability check, most of it was junk. Tyler didn't know much about SSI. He just knew that was how his father had money because he couldn't work.

He could hear his father sleeping in the bedroom. Every so often, he heard his father yell. His dad didn't say specific words. It sounded like he was in pain.

Tyler imagined that his dad was dreaming about the attack on his unit in Afghanistan. His father was one of two survivors.

He wished his dad had never joined the Marines. Tyler used to ask his mom why he did it.

"Why doesn't he want to be with us?" he would ask.

"He wants to be with us." His mom would laugh. "He's away so he can take care of us. Being in the military is going to let him do so many things. They'll pay for him to go to school. Then he can get a really good job."

Tyler's mom had been wrong. The only thing the military had done for his dad was make him crazy.

He put the mail on the table and went over to the couch. Tyler took out his writing journal and started to flip through it. Then he walked out of the unit. He gently closed the door. He made his way to some tables at the back of the complex.

Nobody was ever here. Aside from school, this was the only place Tyler could get away from his life. He wanted to write at a park, but there wasn't one close to his apartment.

Tyler sat down and started writing. His story was about a kid who could stop time. Tyler hadn't worked on the story in a while. He had to reread what he'd already written before going forward. There was so much going on, so many time shifts. Tyler got confused by his own story.

Still, he didn't care. This story was his. He thought it was good, and he didn't care if he ever finished.

Not that he didn't want to. Most of all, Tyler wished he could share his writing with his dad.

Chapter 14

tHROWING IN tHE tOWEL

As much as Tyler wanted to, he didn't talk to Sara on the second day of OCS. The lack of conversation with his father had left him depressed. He had a lot on his mind.

After getting his schoolwork done, Tyler took out his writing journal. This was one of the few times he'd taken it away from home. He never did that. His writing was too important to him. He was afraid he would lose it. This was probably why he never shared it with anybody.

Tyler spent that second day trying to organize his story. He had a good five hours. The only problem was that every time he'd get himself to place where he felt the story made sense, he would come up with a question for the main character that threw everything out of whack.

How could he stop time?

What if he stopped time and couldn't unstop it?

Why was he the only person with this power?

All of these thoughts left Tyler's mind swirling.

Whenever he looked at Sara, she was always doing the same thing. Listening to music on her phone, texting, or staring blankly at the wall. Tyler would've given anything to know what she was thinking.

He didn't dare ask. Tyler didn't want to get yelled at again.

ROUND 3

On Tyler's last day in OCS, there was a new kid in the class. His name was Adrian. He was African American. He was tall and skinny. His hair was cut short. The clothes he wore didn't fit quite right. They looked like hand-me-downs.

Adrian talked a lot. And he was loud. Leon kept telling him to do his work. Adrian would make a smart comment, work for a few seconds, and then start talking again.

Tyler got all his schoolwork done. He took out his journal. He felt all he needed was a few more hours. He could finish outlining the rest of his story in that time. Then he could continue to write.

Tyler didn't normally write like this. He just started with an idea and kept going. He had a lot of unfinished stories. But he didn't care. Writing was his escape. Maybe that's why he left so many things unfinished. It meant he had more places to escape to.

Out of the corner of his eye, Tyler noticed Sara staring at him. He wanted to make a clever comment. He didn't. Adrian had been making those all morning.

"I like to write," Tyler said. "Don't look surprised."

"Anyone can make lines on paper." Tyler loved Sara's voice. Even though she hadn't said one nice thing with it. It was indifferent and expressive all at the same time.

Tyler looked into her dark brown eyes. He smiled and held up his journal. The page was halfway full.

"These aren't just lines."

Sara didn't looked away like she normally did.

"I write too!" Adrian's cocky voice broke into their moment. Tyler wanted to slug him. "You want me to write you a poem, punker girl? A love poem?"

Tyler couldn't help but smile. He may not have been Sara's favorite person to talk to, but she probably thought he was a better option than Adrian.

"I don't want anything from you." Sara looked at her phone.

"Sure you do, punker girl." Adrian smiled. "All right, what kinda guys do you like? What kinda man you interested in?"

Sara rolled her eyes. Tyler figured she was upset that she had even acknowledged him.

"I can tell you're kind of a wild girl. With those things stuck in your face and the clothes you wear," Adrian went on.

Tyler eyed Leon. He was checking his phone. It was like the students weren't even there.

"I know about you punk girls," Adrian started.

"Hey." Tyler's tone was low but stern. "You say another word to her and I'm gonna shut your mouth permanently."

Adrian glanced at Tyler. He laughed.

"You're laughing," Tyler went on. "But that's because you know I'm serious. I don't care that Leon's here."

Leon looked up at them.

"What's the problem?" He tried to sound stern. As if he had been listening to the conversation the whole time.

Adrian laughed Tyler's comments off.

But he barely said a word for the rest of OCS.

Chapter 16

Hope

Tyler walked a few yards behind Sara as the students left school for the day.

He even liked the way she walked. She had confidence. Her head up. Her shoulders back. She had determination. And she seemed to be looking at everything and nothing at once.

He really didn't want to go home. Tyler knew his dad would be there. Sometimes his dad took a shuttle places. Usually it was when he saw his doctors or attended meetings for other wounded veterans. His dad didn't go to those too often.

Tyler couldn't take his eyes off Sara. So he decided to follow her.

Sara made her way across a large strip mall. There was a Ralphs grocery store. Some ethnic food restaurants.

Looking at those, Tyler felt hungry. Due to his family's financial situation, he got a free lunch at school. The only problem was that Tyler thought all school food was gross. He had barely eaten that day.

Sara turned and started walking through an industrial area. There were multiple white buildings. Along them ran a fence that went up to the street.

Tyler wondered where she lived. This seemed like an odd way to go home. He had never been in this area before. Tyler had been so focused on Sara that he didn't exactly know where he was.

And then out of nowhere, Adrian appeared in front of her.

Chapter 17

SAVING SARA

Are they friends? Tyler wondered.

He moved behind one of the white buildings so Adrian couldn't see him following Sara.

Tyler watched as Adrian talked to her. Sara had her arms folded across her chest.

Adrian opened his arms, like he was going to give her a hug. Sara deftly sidestepped him and kept walking. Adrian reached around and grabbed her bag. Sara tried to get it back. Adrian held it up out of her reach.

Tyler started walking over.

Sara didn't seem to notice him until he was a few yards behind Adrian.

"Adrian," Tyler said.

When Adrian turned around, Tyler slugged him in the

face. The punch was clean. Tyler didn't even feel it on his hand.

Adrian fell to the ground.

"Oh, hey!" Adrian said. He held up Sara's bag. "I was just messing around. I didn't know she was your girl."

"I'm not, idiot." Sara glared at both of them and stormed off.

"You punch me and she isn't even your lady?" Adrian smiled.

"Shut up." Tyler walked off after Sara.

Chapter 18

Not Connecting

Tyler was hoping Sara would notice he was behind her. It didn't happen.

He was starting to get mad at himself. Tyler could always talk to girls. He thought about asking her why she was in OCS. He had heard Leon tell her that day that he would see her tomorrow. That meant Sara was going to be in OCS longer than he was.

"You're welcome," he said.

"I didn't tell you to help me." Sara glanced back at him. "And stop following me." She took out her phone. "I'll call the cops."

"And tell them what?" Tyler laughed. "That I saved you from Adrian."

"I didn't need your help."

Tyler was going from mad to furious. No girl had ever gotten to him like this before.

"How come you're in OCS?" he asked.

"I ditched school for a week," Sara started. "They're punishing me for it."

"Why'd you bail for a week?" He figured if he could get her talking, he might be able to break her down a little.

"Because I didn't want to see your ugly face. Just leave me alone! I don't want to talk to you."

Sara's tone was harsh. Her glare was mean. Tyler stopped walking behind her.

She continued on. But the way her body moved, it was like she was almost waiting for him to respond. Like she didn't want to get too far ahead and miss the chance to zing Tyler again.

He wanted to play it cool, but he couldn't.

"You know, you're really beautiful. Your eyes, your hair, your body ... everything. But that doesn't matter because as a person, you suck."

Tyler turned and stormed off in the other direction. He didn't care that she had gotten the best of him. He just wanted his words to hurt her as much as her words hurt him.

"Why'd you follow me?" Sara's voice didn't sound rude anymore. It sounded like she really wanted to know.

Tyler turned around and saw her staring at him.

Chapter 19

PLAY DATE

What does it matter?" he shot back.

"I guess it doesn't." Sara smiled wickedly and started walking away from him again.

He watched her go. Tyler hoped she would turn around without him having to talk first. He knew she wouldn't.

"Where the hell am I?" he asked.

Sara turned and eyed him with a puzzled expression.

"I'm new here. I just transferred from Miller."

"Miller High School? I hear that place blows."

"It wasn't that bad. Anyway, I live in Via Joaquin. Spare me the insults and just tell me how to get back to Banks, please? At least I can get home from there."

He should have been happy. Sara was talking to him. And he could look at her without acting like he wasn't. But he was getting mad.

"Find Via Joaquin on your phone." Sara held up her iPhone.

"I don't have one."

"What? Who doesn't have a phone?"

"I broke mine."

"Get a new one. Duh."

"I can't afford it."

"How'd you break it?"

"I just broke it, okay?"

"Why?" Sara flashed that wicked smile again.

A few minutes before, Tyler would've given anything for Sara's attention. Now he couldn't wait to be done with this conversation.

"Look." He took a deep breath. "You're not gonna help me. You're just gonna mess with me and ask a bunch of lame questions."

"Are you giving up on me?" Sara's voice was a whining now. She even added an over-the-top sad face. "Please don't do that."

Tyler stared at her. He was out of ideas. He had no idea how to respond to this girl. Sara did not fall into any of the typical girl boxes he was used to.

"I can't give you directions." Sara made her voice normal. Her mock sad face disappeared. She looked beautiful to Tyler again. "I barely know my way around. We can use my phone."

Sara walked toward Tyler and kept going. He followed her.

For the moment anyway, they were okay with one another. But Tyler knew she didn't really care if he followed her or not.

Chapter 20

BANTER

So, really?" Tyler asked for probably the fifth time. "You really ditched school for a week?"

"I just didn't feel like going." Sara looked at the ground. "Why do you care anyway? Why are you in OCS?"

"I *was* in OCS. Today was my last day." He glanced at Sara to see if that bothered her.

"Oh."

"Are you gonna miss me?" Tyler smiled.

"No."

They both didn't say anything for a moment.

Tyler hated this. He was used to girls talking. Trying to find out things about him. He did that too, but it was all a game. Tyler was so used to having the upper hand, he didn't know what to say next.

"You think Adrian's still in OCS?" Tyler asked.

"No," Sara started. "I heard Leon and him talking. He was just there because he mouthed off to a teacher the day before."

"I don't remember that." Tyler had thought Sara wasn't paying attention to anything except her phone and her music the whole time.

"You went to the bathroom."

This whole exchange about Adrian was the first time they'd talked without Sara having a sassy comeback.

"Did you miss me?" Tyler decided to push his luck.

"Yeah," Sara stated sarcastically. "I said to myself, 'Where's that idiot who doesn't know anything about good music?'"

"I don't know good music?" Tyler asked.

"EDM isn't music." Sara looked at him. Her expression was serious. Tyler could tell that music was a topic Sara Allen didn't mess around with.

"I told you I know Black Flag."

"And I told you that doesn't mean anything."

"Then why don't you teach me?" Tyler gave Sara his best smile. He didn't listen to music too much. To Tyler, it was just background noise. A way to fill the space.

For Sara, it was a passion. Punk rock was a part of who she was. Tyler envied that.

"Nah." Sara went back to looking around.

Tyler did the same. He saw Banks High School in the distance.

"Well," he said. "You got me back here. I guess your job is done. I can get home now."

"You're dumping me?" Sara smiled. Her smile was so intoxicating, Tyler didn't know if she was really hurt or not.

"I figured that's what you wanted. Thanks for your help." He stopped walking and extended his hand.

Sara half-heartedly slapped it. Her skin was soft. Her touch sent a small jolt through Tyler.

"Let's go." Sara turned around and started walking again.

"To my house?" Tyler couldn't believe it. Minutes before he'd have bet Sara would've walked with anyone other than him.

"Don't sound so excited." She was in front of him now. "I like girls better than guys anyway, Tyler."

Tyler laughed. Sara didn't say anything. He figured she was messing with him. Tyler didn't even care.

Right then, he didn't mind being messed with.

WALKING HOME

As they approached the Via Joaquin apartment complex, Tyler realized this had been a mistake.

He'd been so pumped that Sara wanted to hang out with him. He hadn't realized what having her come over meant.

She would meet his dad.

Tyler knew this could not happen. It wasn't that he was embarrassed. Tyler knew his dad would start something with him.

He could take the abuse when it was just the two of them. For some reason, that was okay. The thought of anybody else seeing it made Tyler's stomach churn.

Sara started doing most of the talking. So far she didn't seemed to notice how quiet Tyler got.

As they walked through the complex, Sara got quiet too. There were only a few people standing around.

One of them was a man Tyler had seen before. He was leaning against the wall with his arms folded. Tyler nodded at him, and the man nodded back. He didn't seem to notice Sara.

The other residents were a man and a woman. The man had his cell phone to his ear. The woman was holding what looked like a utility bill.

"Tell her we already sent the check!" the woman said sternly.

"Would you shut up for a second?" the man shot back at the woman. "She's telling me something."

The man started talking to the person on the phone.

Tyler glanced back at Sara. She was laughing quietly at the exchange. He looked away.

"What?" she asked as they rounded the corner to his apartment.

Tyler shrugged.

"You didn't think that was funny? It was like watching a live-action episode of *Cops*." Sara's smile was wide. Too wide. Tyler couldn't even look at her.

"You wouldn't think it was funny if you had to live here," he stated.

Tyler didn't look at Sara after he said that. He hadn't meant to be mean. Tyler knew he didn't know Sara at all. He didn't want to blow things with her.

They got up to his apartment.

"Why don't you wait outside?" He turned and looked at her. Sara looked up at him with a serious expression. Then she smiled. Their faces with mere inches apart.

"I want to come in." She moved toward the door.

Tyler stood up straight and blocked her with his body.

"Not now."

"Then why did I even come?" Her face looked like it did back in OCS. Tyler was getting nervous that she would bail.

"I'm glad you did. I just can't have you come inside right now." He eyed Sara and hoped that his serious expression would make her understand.

She put her hand on his chest, as if to push him out of the way. Then she slowly ran her hand down it. Tyler held his breath. The electricity was beyond intense.

Sara took a step back. She continued to stare at his chest where her hand had been.

"You're a jock. I guess I can't get past you." She looked at him.

Tyler thought about kissing her. Then he stopped.

"I'm not a jock. I was kicked off the team. I got in a fight. That's why I was in OCS."

"And now you're a writer." Sara made air quotes with her fingers.

"I'm always a writer. Wait here." Tyler held Sara in his gaze as he opened the door to his apartment and went inside.

"Get me something to drink. I'm thirsty," Sara said before he shut the door.

Tyler nodded his head as he turned. He wasn't sure if she saw him or not.

tYLER'S REaLItY
ALL tHE tIME

The first thing Tyler heard was the sound of his dad snoring. Then he saw his father sleeping on the couch. Tyler's bed.

His dad's breathing was heavy enough when he wasn't sleeping. It became truly loud when he was. The sound of air moving through his nose made a squeaking noise as it flowed in and out.

For a brief moment, Tyler remembered when he'd been a little kid. He lived in a small apartment with his mom and dad. Tyler used to mess with his dad as he'd nap. He poured water on him. Tyler would touch his face. His dad would always laugh and then chase Tyler around the house. It was all fun and games.

That was then.

Tyler wouldn't even consider doing something like that now. He didn't even want to think about what his dad might do to him.

Tyler went to the fridge as quietly as possible. There was an open container of juice, an almost finished two-liter bottle of soda, and some small bottles of water. Tyler grabbed one of the water bottles and put it on the table.

He noticed his dad had fallen asleep with the TV on. The volume was turned low. *Walker, Texas Ranger*. Tyler had seen it a few times. He liked it. He wished he could be as Zen as Chuck Norris.

Then Tyler noticed the blanket he usually used was still folded at the end of the couch. He wondered if his dad was warm enough.

Tyler unfolded the blanket and put it on his dad. Then he walked toward the door.

"No blanket!" His dad blinked. He opened his eyes and sat up. "Why'd you wake me?"

"I didn't mean to, Dad." Tyler had to get out of the house before Sara saw or heard his father. "I'll be right back."

"You think you can just walk in and mess with me?"

Tyler put his hand on the doorknob. Instinctively, he ducked.

Good move.

His dad grabbed a coffee cup from the floor and hurled it at him. It shattered against the door.

"Don't mess with me! I'll beat your ass," his dad screamed.

Tyler grabbed Sara's water and opened the door.

Sara's startled expression said it all. This girl who had been messing with him since they met a few days ago actually seemed scared. He took her hand.

"Let's go," he said.

SHARING

†yler and Sara walked out of the complex and onto the street without saying anything.

"Here," Sara said.

She offered Tyler an earbud from her iPhone.

"Who is this?"

"They're a band from England called Sham 69. They've been around forever, and they still play shows."

"What's this song called?"

"'If the Kids Are United.'"

The music had hard, pounding drums, but it wasn't fast in the way that a lot of punk and speed metal songs were. The guitars were crunchy, and the singer sounded like he was singing for his life.

Tyler eyed Sara, who was looking at the ground. She was mouthing all the words as the song played.

Tyler couldn't believe the rush of emotions he felt. Just minutes before he'd almost come to blows with his dad. He was now hanging out with this girl he really liked being around, and she was sharing some of her music with him.

Again, he wanted to kiss her, but he didn't act on it. Tyler knew kissing was no big deal. Sara probably wouldn't think it was a big deal. Already he could tell that she wasn't like other girls. Because of that, he was going to do everything he could not to treat her like just any girl.

Chapter 24

BECAUSE YOU'RE YOUNG

That was cool," Tyler said as he handed Sara back her earbud. They were still walking. He had no idea where they were going, but it seemed like Sara did. Tyler wasn't in any hurry to go home. Sara could take him anywhere.

"They're great. I saw them play in Las Vegas with this band called the Civilians. It was awesome." Sara had lost all the sassiness in her voice. She seemed to be giving Tyler a break. He liked it. But he didn't know how long it was going to last.

"How'd you get out there?" Tyler looked at her.

"My friend Balchack and a bunch of his friends. We did a road trip."

"Cool."

"That's why I was in OCS. The show was on Wednesday. We left on Monday. We didn't get back until Saturday."

Sara looked at Tyler. It was like she was trying to see if he thought she was cool for ditching school.

"Did you get in trouble?"

"Yeah, stupid." Her eyes got wide. "That's why I was in OCS."

"I meant with your parents."

"My parents are idiots. They don't understand me. I just wish they'd leave me alone. I want to become an emancipated minor, but I figure I'll be eighteen soon enough."

"Yeah."

"Was your dad always like that?" Sara looked at Tyler with real interest. Like he had something she wanted. Normally, this would've pissed him off. But Tyler didn't care.

"No. He got hurt in Afghanistan. He was fighting over there. He came back pretty messed up. Then my mom died. That made it worse. It's why we live in that place. We can't afford to live anywhere else."

Sara nodded. She wanted Tyler to continue talking. He did.

Chapter 25

SARA'S REALITY

After talking about Tyler's life, school, music, and politics, they ended up in Sara's neighborhood. Tyler made mental notes of where they were going. He figured he could get home from her house no problem.

Sara's house was in a neighborhood with big homes that all looked the same. They all had small lawns and driveways. And they all looked like mansions to him. Like Adam's house had looked.

"This place sucks." Sara eyed Tyler to see his reaction.

"Well, you've seen where I live." He smiled. "These places look pretty good to me."

"Where you live is real." She was talking with her hands now. "It's the bare essentials. Why do you need any more? If all these people in these McMansions scaled back and donated that money to charity, they could really help people."

"People don't like to give up what they have." Tyler thought Sara didn't appreciate what she had. He hardly had anything. Even when his mom was alive, they were poor and had to get assistance.

They walked up to a big house with two big black cars in the driveway.

"Your McMansion, Madame." Tyler held out his arm toward Sara's house.

"I'm bailing on this place as soon as I can," Sara scoffed.

"Where you gonna go?"

"L.A. I have a lot of friends up there from going to see bands play."

She stared at him with excitement. Tyler looked into her eyes. Something about the wild way she looked at him told him that she was mentally off. Maybe she told him this because she trusted him after spending all day together. Just a little …

"You wanna hang out again?" he asked.

"How will you fit me in?" She smiled. Sara stepped back across the tiny green lawn in front of her house. "All those football games? Pep rallies? Yelling about how excited you are to be in school?"

"I'm not on the team anymore." He frowned.

"So you say. You're probably a double agent."

"Yeah, right," Tyler said. He wanted to insult Sara in a playful way. "Because you're so important."

"I'm not important?" She feigned hurt feelings.

"You are important, Sara." He gave her a serious look and held it. Tyler didn't want any miscommunication about his feelings.

"So tomorrow, huh? I'll think about it." The slyness in Sara's voice ignited a frenzy of emotions within Tyler.

"That's not a no," he said as she opened the door to her parents' big house and went inside.

DATE 2.0

Tyler saw Sara at lunch. She was sitting on a table, tapping her Chuck Taylor's on the bench. She was listening to her iPhone.

He smiled and waved slightly as he went up to her. She didn't smile. She didn't even look at Tyler. She seemed to be thinking about something important. When Tyler was standing right in front of her, she did raise her head slightly in recognition.

"Who you listening to?" he asked.

Sara stared at him blankly. Tyler laughed a little and pointed to her earbuds. Sara took them out of her ears.

"What?" she asked. She hadn't heard anything he said.

"I said 'who are you listening to?'" He continued to smile. Tyler figured that she was messing with him again.

He liked that. It was better than her taking pity on him because of his dad.

"This band from Malaysia." She eyed him. "They're called Roots 'N' Boots. They're playing this Saturday at the Observatory with the Civilians."

"Yes." Tyler took the earbud Sara was holding out.

"Yes, what?" She put the other earbud in her ear.

"Yes, I'll go with you." Tyler sat down next to her.

"I wasn't asking you, dork." Sara smiled a bit after she said that. She continued to look at him. He loved it.

She played Roots 'N' Boots. Tyler thought they were really good. They seemed to have two singers. One who sang melodically. The other one sang more aggressively. Tyler liked them both.

"These guys are awesome," he stated.

Sara smiled. It looked like she believed him. That she knew he wasn't telling her things she wanted to hear.

Tyler saw on Sara's phone that the Roots 'N' Boots song was called "Young, Loud & Proud."

"So what time are we going?" he asked.

Sara turned her iPhone off.

"We aren't going."

"What if I just show up?"

"Show up. I don't care."

Tyler was bummed. It was as if yesterday never happened.

Still, he wasn't going to let it bother him too much. He loved being around her. Tyler loved hearing her voice.

"I'll see you there!" Tyler continued to smile. He waved slightly and walked away from her. Sara seemed surprised.

Tyler looked back. She was still staring at him. Then she looked away.

She's looking, though, he told himself.

Chapter 27

ALONE

Tyler continued walking through school. It was moments like this when he wished he was still on the team. Playing sports gave him instant friends. Tyler could hang out with people even if he didn't know them.

Banks was a big school. When you entered the campus, there was a large plaza with a stage. Classrooms surrounded the plaza. If you kept walking, you found more classrooms, more open spaces, a newly built science building, and then the large field and gymnasium.

Tyler missed being on that field. Even though he hadn't played football for long, he'd enjoyed being a part of something. His counselor had recommended that he play. The school even covered the costs of the uniform and gear.

For a moment, Tyler was filled with a tinge of regret.

What if I hadn't hit Adam? he asked himself. *What if I had just walked away?*

Tyler knew it wasn't possible. Not for him or Adam.

They would have always had a problem. Adam never would've let go of what Tyler did with Cassie. Kissing. It was no big deal to Tyler.

Tyler wouldn't have been able to stand what Adam dished out.

And that was the problem. People like Adam could afford to dish it out. It didn't matter how they took it.

Tyler didn't have the luxury.

He made his way back to the front of the school. Tyler knew lunch would be ending soon. His next class, English, was right there. If he was lucky, he might pass Sara.

Maybe he'd get a smile.

If nothing else, they'd make eye contact. At least Tyler wouldn't feel so alone.

"So this is where people with no friends go," Tyler heard a voice say.

He saw Adam standing with Donovan and Anthony. Anthony was another player on the football team. Tyler remembered somebody on the team telling him that Anthony was tough.

Tyler didn't care.

HATERS

Adam, Donovan, and Anthony watched as Tyler approached.

Tyler was big, like they were. He walked with the same strength and confidence. Had things not happened with Cassie, he probably would've been tight with them. Tyler knew how to party. He liked to have a good time. He would've fit right in with Adam and his crew.

"You know who I saw him talking to?" Tyler overheard Donovan ask. "Sara Allen."

Anthony laughed. "That's because nobody's told him she's crazy."

They laughed.

"I like crazy," Adam finally said. "Sara's kinda hot, right?"

Tyler squeezed his fists as he walked past them. He did his best to think about something else. He told himself not to think about what they were saying. He didn't want to hear it.

He could feel their eyes burn into his back.

Chapter 29

MR. ZAMORA

As the students filed out from fifth period and headed to sixth, Tyler heard his English teacher, Mr. Zamora, call his name.

"Can I talk with you for a minute?" Mr. Zamora was sitting at his desk, working on his laptop.

What now? Tyler wondered.

Had he blown a writing assignment? Had he not followed directions? English had always been his best subject. The last thing he needed was to have problems in his favorite class.

"What's up?" Tyler tried not to sound defensive, but he couldn't help it. He had always been told that he looked for fights. But he was getting older. He couldn't do that anymore.

"I wanted to talk to you about one of your assignments." Mr. Zamora reached into his files to get one of Tyler's papers.

As he did, Tyler looked around the room. Mr. Zamora played guitar in a band called Weird Science. He had pictures of Mozart, Bach, the Beatles, and Led Zeppelin posted around the classroom.

From what Tyler could tell, Mr. Zamora always wore a sweater and a tie. The teacher kept his class real loose. As long as the students did their work, they could listen to music on their phones. They could even text.

"How come you're in this class?" Mr. Zamora pulled out Tyler's paper. It was a writing assignment Tyler did when he was in OCS. It was a one-page reflection on the best moment of his life.

Tyler had written about the one time he'd gone to Disneyland with his mother and father.

"Your writing is honor's level," Mr. Zamora went on. "You're gonna be bored out of your mind in here."

Tyler couldn't believe what he was hearing. Nobody had ever really commented on the work he did. If they did, they were usually being super-critical. This was probably why Tyler didn't do his homework as often as he should. It was easier to get Ds and just pass than it was to deal with teachers.

"I like your class," Tyler stated.

"I can put you in my honor's class." Mr. Zamora smiled at him. He seemed to see something in Tyler. Something that nobody in his life saw. He thought Tyler was good at something. Writing.

"Aren't honor's kids all snobs?" Mr. Zamora laughed after Tyler asked that. Tyler frowned.

"Some are ... but you'll also challenge yourself in there. This class will be way below where you're at academically."

"I think it's better if I just stay here. Around people who are more like me."

"You don't want to push yourself?" Mr. Zamora smiled when he asked that. Tyler could tell he wasn't dissing him. Not like that other teacher at his old school.

"It's not that. I seem to have problems all the time. I just want to lie low for a while. Get by ..." Tyler let his words trail off.

"You can stay in this class." Mr. Zamora stood up. "I'm not going to force you out or anything. But I'd like you to consider doing more than just getting by. Okay, Tyler?"

Chapter 30

FIRSt SHOW

Tyler was glad that he'd remembered the name of the club where Sara had told him the show would be. The Observatory. He Googled its location in the library during lunch.

Surprisingly, it was only about four miles from his house. Tyler decided to walk there.

The Observatory was a large brick building. Around it were offices as well as industrial buildings. There were people in the parking lot. Other people lined up to get inside.

People were wearing denim jackets with patches on them. The patches had names of bands like the Exploited, Crass, and Infest. Other people wore tight jeans, boots, and Fred Perry shirts. A lot of the guys and girls had shaved heads. A few of the girls had their hair styled the same way as Sara.

Tyler wore jeans and a black T-shirt. It didn't say anything on it. He didn't think he looked out of place. The only different thing about him was that he was alone. Everybody seemed to be with someone.

As he watched people paying to get in, he had sick feeling in his stomach.

He had no money on him.

Tyler had fifteen dollars that he was holding on to for as long as he could. But it was back at the apartment. His dad had given it to him a couple months ago. Most of the time Tyler went without cash.

There was a white piece of paper in the box office window with the entrance fee written on it in big black letters: $10. Tyler felt like punching himself. He hadn't even thought to bring his money. For some reason he thought that punk rockers didn't charge when their bands played. He told himself not to tell Sara about this. She would think he was dumber than she already did.

He didn't know what to do. He could hear the music. But it sounded like noise. He figured it probably sounded better inside. That's where Sara was. Tyler knew that no matter what he had to get into the club.

As he stood there, a bald guy in a gray flight jacket, tight black jeans, and combat boots walked up to him. He didn't say anything. He just stared at Tyler.

"What's up?" Tyler asked.

"Not much," the person said. "I thought you were somebody else."

"Oh."

"My name's Balchack," the person said. He extended his hand.

Tyler shook it. Then he remembered that Sara had mentioned somebody named Balchack.

"You're Sara's friend!" Tyler tried not to sound as excited as he was. Maybe he had a chance to get into the club. At the very least, Sara would know he was outside.

"Sara?" Balchack seemed confused. "Oh, you mean Birdy." Balchack smiled and lit a cigarette.

"Yeah," Tyler started. "She has a shaved head, wears skinny jeans, and band T-shirts."

"You could be describing all the girls in the club!" Balchack laughed.

"My name's Tyler."

"So Birdy knows you're here?" Balchack seemed surprised.

Are they together? Maybe Balchack likes her.

The last thing Tyler wanted was to have any problems with anyone tonight. He just wanted to see Sara. To see the expression on her face when he walked into her world.

"Kinda." Tyler was choosing his words carefully. "She told me about the show. We met at school. She's been playing me some of the music."

"So this is your first show?" Balchack beamed.

"Yeah."

"Well then." Balchack started walking. He motioned for Tyler to come with him. "Let's get you inside. The Civilians will be on soon."

"Okay." Tyler followed Balchack. "But I don't have …"

Tyler stopped talking as he watched Balchack shake a bunch of hands. Seemed like Balchack knew a lot of people.

They got up to the bouncer. Tyler took a deep breath. He was embarrassed about not having any money.

"What's up, Soto?" Balchack waved at the bouncer.

Soto smiled. He opened the door.

"He's with me." Balchack motioned to Tyler. "He's friends with Birdy."

A big grin came over Soto's face. Tyler wondered what that meant.

Was this all a joke? Was Sara hoping he'd show up so she could mess with him? Did a lot of guys come to punk shows because of her?

"Thank you," Tyler said to Soto. He followed Balchack into the Observatory.

UNDERGROUND YOUTH CULTURE

†yler was glad he dressed lightly. The Observatory was hot and filled with people. After walking up a ramp and through many people, Tyler followed Balchack into the main room. The band the Authority was playing a loud set. Tyler only knew this was the band's name because it was written across the drummer's bass.

The Authority was fast, and the audience seemed to really like them. The crowd was moving around in a frenetic circle.

This must be the pit, Tyler told himself. It didn't look too scary, but he wasn't sure he wanted to go in there. He wanted to watch it a little more so he'd know what he was doing.

Balchack waded through a sea of people wearing shirts for bands like Descendants, Dead Kennedys, and Cockney Rejects. Eventually, they got to a side area where Sara was watching the band with some friends.

Tyler didn't want to acknowledge his presence immediately. It wasn't because he was scared. He didn't want to ruin the moment for Sara. As she watched the band, she had a huge smile on her face. Sara looked happy.

Tyler had seen Sara smile before, but this was different. It was as if she felt more comfortable in this club, with these people and this music, than she did anywhere else in the world.

"There she is, man!" Balchack patted Tyler on the shoulder.

"Yeah." Tyler nodded his head.

Sara looked over at him. She stared at him for a moment. Then her eyes got really big. She almost started to smile at him, but she caught herself.

Tyler walked over to her.

"I told you I was coming." He smiled a little bit. "Your friend Balchack got me in."

"I can't believe you're actually here, listening to music that's real and not electronic," she said flatly.

Tyler wondered if she was mad. Like he wasn't supposed to come into her world unless she was leading the way.

"You're really here." She smiled again.

Tyler eyed the three people Sara was standing with.

"This is Tyler." She motioned to him. Sara pointed to her friends. Because the music was so loud, she had to lean in close to talk in his ear. Tyler could feel her hair sweep against his face. "This is Laura, Hartsfield, and Doc."

"Hi." Tyler waved.

He noticed they were all dressed the same. Black clothes. Short hair.

Laura wore a shirt that said GBH. Hartsfield's said sXe, meaning straight edge, on the pocket. Doc's shirt said Yuck-mouth across the chest.

They greeted him.

Sara smiled at Tyler and went back to watching the band.

Chapter 32

Sara's Turf

The Civilians were playing. The drums were pounding. The strong guitars and in-your-face vocals whipped the pit into a frenzy.

"This place doesn't look so tough." Tyler stated as he and Sara stood off to the side. She was standing in front of Tyler. He had to lean down to whisper in her ear.

There was something about how they were standing that he loved. Tyler didn't know if the reason he felt so good was only because of Sara. He didn't know if it was the way he could see the nape of her neck. Tyler didn't know if it was how close they were. He just felt happy and proud to be with her.

"I love this place." Sara stared in awe at the power the Civilians had over the crowd. "You can be anybody you want here. It's not like high school where everybody judges you all the time."

"I never even knew this place existed before tonight." Tyler laughed.

"I think the owner has the hots for me. Dominic always lets me in for free. I've even hung out here during the day when there's nothing going on." Sara glanced at Tyler.

"What do you do when you're here alone?"

"Wouldn't you like to know." Sara smiled at him.

"Why do your friends call you Birdy?" Tyler asked.

At that moment, Balchack, Hartsfield, and Doc ran over and grabbed Tyler. He eyed Sara, who smiled at him.

Is this a setup? he wondered. *Why would these people be messing with me right now. They seemed so cool.*

" 'Side by Side,' " Balchack said. "You gotta dance to this song."

Before Tyler knew what was going on, he was being ushered toward the tornado of bodies known as the slam pit.

Chapter 33

tHE PIt

With Hartsfield in front of him and Balchack and Doc behind, Tyler burst into the pit like a car on a fast-moving freeway.

Instinctively, Tyler started throwing his arms around. He was bashing into people, much like how he would if he was on the football field. Tyler was going so fast he didn't notice the angry looks from the other people around him.

This went on for a moment until Balchack grabbed him.

"Dude," Balchack's voice was stern. "Dial it back! It's not about mowing people down. You're in the inner circle. You're part of the energy by releasing your own. Stop throwing elbows!"

Balchack let go of Tyler. They started moving around the pit together. The pulsating rhythms of "Side By Side" from the Civilians were nonstop. Tyler couldn't believe how close the crowd was to the band. Everything they were giving off onstage was being given back with equal fervor from the pit.

In a heartbeat, Tyler understood why this scene made Sara feel so alive. He couldn't believe how moved he was by the power of the music.

The song stopped. The singer yelled things to the crowd; they yelled things back. Everybody was laughing and having a good time.

Tyler stood with Balchack, Hartsfield, and Doc. He was really sweaty but so was everybody else. He looked around and spotted Sara.

She was listening to the banter between the singer and the audience. Sara still had a big smile on her face. Tyler thought she was looking at him.

BIRD TROUBLE

Roots 'N' Boots, a Malaysian Oi band, was playing. The crowd was energized. The pit area was full. Tyler couldn't even get close to it. He stood off to the side. He wanted to go back where Sara was, but he didn't want to crowd her too much.

Balchack walked over. He held two plastic cups.

"Thought you might be needing this." He smiled. "It's water."

"Thanks." Tyler took a large drink from his cup. The water was cold. He'd released so much adrenaline during the Civilians set. He hadn't realized how thirsty he was.

"So how'd you start talking to Birdy?" Balchack turned to watch Roots 'N' Boots.

"We were both suspended. It was on campus. Three days. She didn't start talking to me until after the first two days passed. She told me she got in trouble because she went to a show or something." Tyler took another sip of his water.

"Oh yeah." Balchack continued to watch the band. "Look, Tyler, there's no cool way to say this, so I'm just going to say it. Myself, Hartsfield, Laura, Doc, all of Birdy's friends … we love her. So I'm just telling you to be cool with her. She doesn't always make that easy."

Tyler and Balchack looked at each other. The old Tyler would fight. But things were different. There would be no argument tonight.

"Of course." Tyler wanted to be as cool as possible. He wanted Sara's friends to know he really cared about her. "Were you guys ever together?"

"Yeah, for like half a second." Balchack laughed. "She's like my sister. I just … I don't know what you know. But she's kinda messed up in the head."

"Aren't all girls?" Tyler was trying to play it too cool, and he knew it. He'd never had a conversation with another guy like this before. Especially when that other guy wasn't interested in the girl.

"Tyler." Balchack wasn't laughing, but he wasn't mad. He wanted Tyler to know he was serious. "She's *really* messed up. Like she takes meds for it. I think she told me she was bi-polar."

"Oh." Tyler didn't really understand. His dad took

meds, but all they did was make him sleep. When he was awake … Tyler didn't want to think about his dad tonight.

"I know you'll treat her right. I think she likes you." Balchack continued to watch the band.

Tyler nodded his head. He wanted to find Sara.

"You know where she is?"

"I think I saw her by the bar."

"Thanks." Tyler made his way over.

The bar was packed with people. They weren't ordering drinks. Many of them were just standing in front of it, rocking out to Roots 'N' Boots.

The song "Young, Loud & Proud" was next. This was the song that Sara had played for him.

As Tyler looked around, he saw two girls off to the side of the bar. They were making out. Nobody was paying any attention to them.

Nobody except Tyler.

When they pulled away, Tyler saw that one of the girls was Sara. She smiled at the girl she was kissing. They turned and watched the band. Sara didn't see Tyler staring at her.

Tyler felt like his insides were exploding. Sara had been keeping him on his toes. He hadn't expected anything like this.

It was too much.

Tyler left the Observatory. The energizing music from this new world trailed off behind him.

Chapter 35

ESCAPE

It was almost one in the morning by the time Tyler got home. The last thing he wanted to deal with was his dad. Normally he could take it. Tyler could take anything.

Not tonight.

During the walk home, he was trying to figure out how he had let Sara play him.

She just thinks I'm a joke, he kept telling himself.

Tyler was even angrier with himself.

Why did I care so much?

He had never let a girl do something like this to him. Sure, not every girl had been in love with him, but none had ever affected him the way Sara did.

Tyler hated that she could make him feel good *and* bad. It was something Sara had in common with his father.

The biggest difference was that Tyler *wanted* to be

around Sara. He couldn't explain why. He didn't even know her, really. But nobody had ever made him feel so many things at once. He knew he'd be willing to take her abuse if it meant he'd get closer to her.

But then, Sara liked girls.

Tyler was just a fun diversion for her. She didn't take him seriously.

I actually thought I broke her down. He was in full pity mode now. *Pathetic. I actually thought she liked me. Well, no more.*

Tyler swore to himself that he was never going to talk to her again.

"She thinks she can just keep messing with me. Well, she doesn't even exist to me anymore."

Tyler looked around the apartment. He heard his father sleeping. It sounded like he was talking to someone in whatever dream he was having. Tyler used to listen to him. Then his dad woke up, caught him, and got angry.

Tyler was starting to get angry. He wasn't supposed to be in the apartment. He wanted to be out with Sara. He didn't want to be alone. Before he let his thoughts start to suffocate him, he grabbed his journal and left the apartment.

Tyler went out to the dimly lit tables. His writing spot. The one place that was his. He was nervous there might be people around. Sometimes on Saturday nights, people liked to hang out there and drink. Thankfully, it was deserted.

As Tyler opened up his writing journal, he thought about how much he wanted to be like the character in his story. If he could've stopped time, he wouldn't have left the club. He would have gone over to Sara, made time go again, and yelled at her. Just as she was about to respond, Tyler would've stopped time again so he could leave without having to hear her voice.

Oh well, he told himself. *I'm never gonna hear it again now. I've got nothing to say to her.*

As Tyler tried to write, he became frustrated. He couldn't stop thinking about Sara. He wasn't even thinking about her with the other girl. He couldn't stop seeing her face.

Smiling as she watched the bands. The enthusiasm in her eyes. The way she looked at him as he leaned in to talk to her at the Observatory.

Tyler had felt so good at the show. He liked the music. Sara's friends were cool. She was happy he was there.

And that's when Tyler realized what was bumming him out the most. For the first time in a very long time, he felt like he belonged somewhere.

Wrong, like always.

Still, despite how bad he felt. Despite not being able to write. Tyler couldn't stop picturing Sara's face.

And it made him feel good.

†HE SWINGS

Tyler was cleaning the apartment when there was a knock on the door. This surprised him. Nobody ever knocked on the door. Nobody ever visited. Tyler's dad took a shuttle to his appointments. But it just waited at the front of the apartment complex. If a friend picked him up, Tyler's dad met them out front too. That's what his dad had done this morning when he got a ride to church.

The knocking continued.

Tyler put down the paper towel and spray cleaner. He'd been dusting the coffee table. He answered the door.

Sara was standing there. She wore a gray tank top with suspenders, jeans, and combat boots.

Tyler couldn't believe she was there. He also couldn't believe she continued to look better and better.

"Aren't you going to invite a lady in?" She smiled like everything was okay.

"Sure." He took several steps back from the door. Tyler wasn't sure when his dad would be home. But he didn't think Sara would be there long.

Sara walked in.

Dissing girls. Not talking to them when they wanted to be talked to. Ignoring them. Tyler understood this part of the game.

But Sara was so outside of his world. He knew this was going to be hard.

He was going to have to be a jerk.

"Are you gonna give me a tour?" She was more bubbly than she'd ever been.

She must know I'm angry, he thought. *Maybe she feels bad. Who cares! I don't want her pity.*

"This is the living room." He quickly pointed around the apartment. "That's my dad's bedroom. That's the bathroom. Kitchen's over there, as you can see."

"Where's your bedroom?" Sara eyed him. Tyler had to look away. He couldn't give in.

"You're in it." He pretended like he was cleaning something off the table.

"So I'm in your bed right now?" Sara's voice sounded seductive as she sat down on the couch.

"I don't know." Tyler moved into the kitchen and turned on the faucet. There were a few dishes in the sink.

"Is this another one of your stories?" Sara held up Tyler's journal.

"Yeah."

"What's it about?" She started leafing through the pages.

"A kid who can stop time."

"That sounds cool." Sara seemed to read through it.

Tyler stole a glance of her. She looked amazing sitting on the couch.

Why did she have to come over now? I don't get it.

"You wanna go for a walk?" Sara asked. "Or we can go for a drive. I got my mom's car." Sara put Tyler's writing journal down.

"Sure." Tyler shrugged.

He didn't know how long he was going to be able to keep this cool act going. But he knew he had to. Too bad this all only made him like Sara more.

Chapter 37

†HE DEAL

†yler and Sara walked for a while. She talked the whole time. Tyler stared at the ground, cars, and buildings. Sara was being funny. Or she was trying to be. She seemed to sense something was on Tyler's mind, but she didn't say anything.

They walked a long way and found a park. There was a swing set, some monkey bars, a slide, plus some benches. Everything was really old and riddled with graffiti. This wasn't the kind of park Tyler would want to write in.

"Why are you being weird?" Sara finally asked.

"Sorry." Tyler kicked a rock.

"I don't owe you anything, if that's what you're thinking." Sara's tone was no longer playful. She had him in her sights, but Tyler could only glance at her. It hurt too much. "You can't say I wasn't up front. I told you I liked girls."

He stared at her.

"I saw you looking at me all hurt and surprised after I kissed Leslie."

"You talk too much … " Tyler started. He wanted to be cool and control himself. That's how Tyler Ruiz always was around the opposite sex. But he was tired of being cool. "I have no idea when you're serious or being real. I like you, okay?"

Tyler met Sara's firm gaze head-on. He wasn't going to look away for anything.

"You thought I was just a jock. Well, I thought you were some weird punk girl. You're much more than that, Sara. And I hate that I know that because I can't just be okay with you. I can't ever look at you the same way again. Do you have any idea how hard it is to be around you and not be with you?"

"I'm not that great, Tyler." Sara couldn't even look at him as she said it. "You hang out with me long enough, you'll realize that."

"Why don't you let me figure that out for myself? You're always so busy being defensive and shutting me down. All that does is make me want to be with you even more."

Sara stared hard into his eyes after he said it.

"But you already know that," he said.

Sara leaned in and put her hands on Tyler's shoulders.

Then she kissed him. It wasn't hard. It wasn't soft. It was just how he liked it. Tyler wanted to wrap his arms around her and bask in everything Sara meant to him, but he was nervous. He thought it might scare her.

"I was serious," she said. She pulled away. She moved back and climbed up to sit on one of the park's dirty metal tables. "I like girls and guys. I know that's not what a guy like you typically expects."

Tyler sat down beside her. "What do you think I expect?" He forced himself to smile. Tyler didn't want to be too serious. He knew he still needed to be cool.

"You know: a wife, two kids, a big house. The girl next door. That's not me."

"I think you're getting ahead of yourself." He kissed her again. He noticed that her lip piercing didn't get in the way. He had never kissed a girl who had one. "I'm not exactly the guy next door, right?"

She wrapped her arms around his neck. He loved how soft her skin was. How soft she was. He wrapped his arms around her.

"Let's go," Sara whispered. "Right here."

Tyler pulled back.

"What? We can't do it here." He smiled.

"You're such a jerk!" Sara pushed him away.

Then she hopped off the table and stormed off.

"Sara!" Everything happened so fast Tyler couldn't

process it. They were having a great make-out session. Now she hated him again.

"Don't follow me!" she yelled at the top of her lungs. "You're just a jock!"

Tyler continued walking after her. He slowed his pace because people in the park were looking at them.

"Stay away! Stay away!" she yelled.

Sara then turned and eyed him. She started to laugh. It was big and loud. She had fire in her eyes. It scared Tyler.

Then she ran off, leaving Tyler alone once again.

Good Looking Out

Tyler looked for Sara at the first break. Then at lunch. Then in the time between classes.

He couldn't find her.

School ended for the day. Tyler continued looking for her. As he walked around Banks High School for the umpteenth time, he finally spotted her standing under a tree.

Then he realized why he had missed her all day.

Sara had changed her hair. It was jet black now and shorter. Tyler still thought she looked amazing. She just looked different enough for him not to notice her right away.

Tyler went over to her. Sara looked at him, but she didn't seem to see him.

Is she doped up on meds? Tyler wondered.

"Hey," he said.

Sara raised her eyebrows to acknowledge that he had said something. But that was all she did.

"How was your day?" Tyler felt like an idiot asking, but Sara wasn't giving him anything to work with.

She started walking away. Tyler felt like he could disappear and it wouldn't mean anything to her.

Tyler caught up to her. "Do people only have a few days a month to be friends with you?" he blurted out. "I think I've known you for two weeks, and you've hated me for most of it."

Sara looked at him. Then she looked away.

She burst out laughing. Tyler couldn't help smiling. He was just happy to have broken through, even for just a moment.

"Look, I wasn't rejecting you," he went on. "I like you. A lot. I just … you're just so different than any other girl I've known."

"Why? Because I like having sex?" She glared at him. Tyler had never had this kind of a frank talk with a girl.

"No … it's just, you like girls and guys. Saturday night you were making out with that one girl."

"Leslie." Sara smiled a bit. Tyler did not like the direction the conversation was taking.

"Then the next day you're making out with me," he went on.

"And? You can't deal with that?"

"I don't *just* want to have sex with you. I actually want to get to know you."

They both stopped walking. They stared at each other. Somehow, Tyler could tell by Sara's eyes that she believed him. That he really did want more than sex.

"Well," Sara said. "My name is Sara. With no *h*. I like slasher movies and Dean Koontz novels. I'm Aquarius. I go to Banks High School, but you knew that. I like music that's hard, fast, and loud."

Tyler couldn't help but grin as Sara continued to rattle off information about herself.

"I don't like onions, but I will eat them if they are part of the overall food experience. I might go to college. I want to help people."

With her index finger she motioned for him to come closer.

Before he knew what was happening, he fell into her embrace. They started to kiss again. It wasn't as fast or frenetic as the first time. It didn't need to be. This one was warm, slow, and good.

Tyler couldn't believe this was happening again. He opened his eyes. He wanted to see Sara's face. To see if she was looking at him.

She wasn't. Her eyes were closed.

Before Tyler closed his, he saw Adam and some of the

other football players practicing on the field. Coach was running drills with the defense. The offensive players were getting into position. Adam looked at Tyler. There was a sneer on his face.

Tyler closed his eyes quickly. He wasn't going to let Adam ruin any more moments for him.

CLOSER

Tyler was trying not to laugh, but he couldn't help it. Sara had connected her phone to an iHome device. The song playing was by Tom Waits. He kept singing "goodnight, Irene" over and over.

Tyler couldn't believe anybody would willingly listen to that man sing.

"You just don't like good music," she stated as she ran her fingers through Tyler's hair.

They were lying on her bed. Tyler had wanted to wait before being with her. Things just happened too fast. He couldn't control himself, and Sara certainly wasn't making it any easier.

Her room was a mess. Clothes were strewn everywhere. Books, CDs, and vinyl records were stacked on shelves. She had plastered the walls with flyers from punk shows. A screensaver with the band name Combat 84 moved across her laptop screen.

"How come you got in a fight when you were on the football team?"

Tyler looked at Sara.

"I got in a fight with this guy Adam." Tyler looked at Sara's gray bedsheet. "I guess you can't be on the team if you have a beef with him."

"I meant, what'd you guys fight about, dork? Who looks better in those tight white football pants?" Sara laughed.

"His girlfriend. I think she was trying to mess with him. Make him jealous or something. I didn't even do anything with her, really. I was at a party at his house. I bailed after that, and then he got in my face the next day."

"So what are you gonna do now?" Sara seemed genuinely curious. She didn't seem like she was asking that question just to make another one of her sly comments.

"I'm gonna date a hot punk girl."

"I'm a skinhead."

"Excuse me." Tyler tried to sound official. "A skinhead."

They stared at one another. He knew he could do this for hours. Tyler knew it would be very easy to lose himself with Sara. He felt vulnerable.

And he didn't care.

"Why do they call you Birdy?"

"That's a skinhead thing. It's what they call the skin-head girls."

"You don't think that's kinda demeaning? To call a girl a bird?"

"It's better than being called someone's babe or their old lady."

Tyler laughed.

"I like it." Sara looked up at the ceiling. "Birds are free. Like I wanna be."

A noise came from downstairs. Sara's parents were home.

Chapter 40

THE 'RENTS

Before Tyler knew what was happening, he was on the street in front of Sara's house. His exit had been just like one of those '80s movies he'd seen on YouTube.

Tyler quickly got dressed. Then he climbed out Sara's window onto the roof. From there, he moved as quickly and quietly as possible until he dropped to the grass at the side of the house.

Tyler spotted her parents through the front window as he walked past their big house. Their expensive cars were parked in the driveway. But Tyler didn't think they looked like snobs.

Sara's mom had long curly hair. She wore a dress and just seemed like the mom of a teenage girl. Her dad wore a sweater and jeans. He had a short beard. They certainly looked nothing like his parents.

As Tyler got farther from her house, he got an uneasy feeling. On the one hand, he had just been with a girl he really liked. On the other, what if she was embarrassed by him? Until now, Tyler never cared.

I got what I wanted, he would've told himself. *I'm cool. Where's the next one?*

But Tyler didn't feel that way at all now. He couldn't wait to see Sara again. She had fast become the only person he even cared about seeing.

What if this was it?

What if Sara used me? What if all she wanted was sex?

Tyler couldn't wrap his head around it. Thoughts were coming too fast.

"Calm down, bro," he said out loud. Tyler knew he was too inside his own head.

Out of nowhere, a large black car pulled up behind him. Tyler jumped back.

"What's up?" Tyler said to whoever was in the car. He couldn't see who it was, but his first instinct was that it was Adam and some of the other football players.

†HE †RU†H?

Is that how you get hard with people?" Sara rolled down the car's window. A punk band was blasting from the sound system. She was smoking a cigarette.

Tyler smiled and got inside.

"Sorry about having you bail like that." Sara took a drag on her cigarette. She offered it to Tyler, but he shook his head. "My parents are just weird. They don't understand me at all. They totally want me to date rich guys and people who come from rich families."

Tyler nodded his head. He didn't know what to say to that. He and Sara both had problems with their parents. To Tyler, Sara's problems sounded easy.

"They would totally hold where you're from against you," she added. "This is why I am how I am. I want nothing—nothing—to do with any of their two-point-two kids, white picket fence, perfect family crap. It's all fake. All of it."

"They'd love me if they met me." Tyler was trying to lighten the mood. He didn't know Sara that well, but he knew when she was keyed up.

Sara laughed, but he could tell she didn't agree with him.

"They have me take pills. They say the way I act isn't normal. Well, I'm not normal compared to those fakers. I don't want to be normal like them."

Story

Tyler was scribbling furiously at his writing spot in the apartment complex. Normally, writing came easy for him. Today, the words were flowing even better than usual. Tyler was inspired in a way he'd never been before.

He was writing a story for Sara. At first, he was going to call it "Sara Smile." His dad used to listen to that song by Hall and Oates when Tyler was little. He used to listen to Phil Collins too.

Ever since he got back from Afghanistan, his dad didn't listen to music. Tyler wondered if everything he heard reminded him of his dead wife.

One time in their old apartment, Tyler put on the song "In the Air Tonight." Tyler's dad got so mad Tyler left the apartment. He didn't come back until it was time for school the next morning. He was thirteen.

His story for Sara would be called "Skinhead Chick." Sara always talked like it was her against the world. So he made her a superhero. The Skinhead Chick helps people who can't help themselves. She fights for the abused, the outcasts, and anyone else who's suffering.

It was almost eleven o'clock. Tyler knew he needed to get to bed soon. The problem was, he knew he wouldn't be able to fall asleep.

Sara had inspired him in a way he'd never thought possible. He was going to write till he either fell asleep outside or the story was done. Either way, he didn't care.

Tyler was just happy to be doing something for the girl he was falling in love with.

Making a Mark

†yler, you know I'll read anything you write." Mr. Zamora smiled as he opened his lunch.

Class had just ended. Tyler told his teacher about "Skinhead Chick." He didn't tell Mr. Zamora that Sara was his girlfriend or anything. He just said they were hanging out.

"I just write a lot. Not school assignments. I don't know if it's any good or not," Tyler stated.

"You ever ask your parents for feedback?" Mr. Zamora cracked open a Diet Coke.

Tyler shook his head. "My dad … he doesn't care about me. At least not what I write."

"What about your mom?" Mr. Zamora seemed to know not to ask too many questions. He also acted like it wasn't a big deal so Tyler wouldn't feel awkward.

"Mom's dead."

"Show me 'Skinhead Chick.' Can I read any of it now?"

"No." Tyler eyed the computers against the wall in the room. "It's all longhand. Would it be cool if I typed it up here when it's done?"

"Sure. I eat lunch in here, and I usually stay here for a few hours after school."

"Thanks. I might start today, but I'll probably start tomorrow."

Tyler left Mr. Zamora's room.

As he walked to sixth period, he saw the football team boarding the bus for an away game. Tyler hardly cared, and he felt good about it. So he'd been kicked off the team. It just gave him more time to write.

Tyler was also happy about Mr. Zamora. For the first time since his mom died, he felt there was actually another adult who gave a damn about him.

Chapter 44

SIDED

✝yler got home. He noticed that his dad wasn't there. This was odd because it was Thursday. His dad was almost always home on Thursdays.

He quickly started his schoolwork. Tyler wanted to get that done and get to work on "Skinhead Chick" as soon as possible. He'd had ideas all day. He wanted to write them down so he didn't forget them.

First up was math. The class was easy. Tyler thought maybe he should say something. He didn't want to be in basic classes his whole life. Administrators just placed him there. He figured they did that because the work was easy. Tyler could get it done. He could do well, and then he wouldn't get angry. If he wasn't getting angry, then he wasn't a problem. If Tyler wasn't a problem, then nobody had to deal with him.

As he finished his work, he wondered what was on TV. He rarely watched. He tried to be in the apartment as little as possible. Everybody in school was always talking about what they watched on TV or YouTube. Tyler usually had nothing to say.

He began his last assignment: science questions. He started to really like the idea of not leaving the apartment to write. Not having to deal with the other residents of Via Joaquin for one night.

Then the door opened. Tyler's dad walked in. He was carrying a McDonald's bag and a drink. Tyler could tell by the bag's size that his dad hadn't thought to get him anything.

No problem, Tyler said to himself. He tried not to look at his dad. *I can take care of myself.*

Tyler wasn't a great cook. He could make things like pasta and sandwiches.

More than anything, he wanted his dad to take his food into his bedroom. Tyler just wanted to be left alone. He wanted get to work on "Skinhead Chick." Working on that made him feel connected to Sara when they were apart.

Tyler was so focused on science, he didn't notice his dad getting closer. That's when his father slapped him in the face.

It was a hard slap that stung. Tyler wasn't sure if it hurt more because he wasn't expecting it, or because he couldn't believe his dad would actually do that to him for no reason.

You should be used to this by now, he told himself.

The fact was, Tyler still thought there was some part of his father in there. That the person inside his dad's body wasn't a complete monster.

"I know you're planning something." His dad raised his hand like he was going to hit Tyler again. "You're just like those people over there. They pretend to be busy. They pretend to be normal. That's when they get you."

His dad brought his hand down again. That's when Tyler grabbed his father's arm and stood up.

They were face-to-face now.

They were close. Tyler could smell the french fries on his father's breath. His dad's face dropped a bit. It was like he was waiting for something. Like he wanted to Tyler to hit him.

Why?

So he could throw him out of the house? So he could feel something again instead of being doped up on meds?

Tyler let go of his dad's arm. He pushed him back a bit. Tyler wanted distance between them. He wanted to be ready if his dad tried anything like that again.

Tyler bent down and picked up his homework. He grabbed his journal with his stories. That was all he really needed. That was all Tyler Ruiz cared about in this small apartment.

"I'm going outside." Tyler didn't even look at his dad.

Tyler didn't know when their next confrontation would be. He just knew there would be definitely be another one.

SHELL-SHOCKED

Tyler finished his science homework. As he stared at "Skinhead Chick," he was mad. His dad had sapped all of his inspiration. He hated that he could do that.

Tyler looked at his hand. Then he stared at his pencil. Like a camera focusing, the tip came into sharp view. Then it went out of focus. Tyler knew why.

His hand was shaking.

Suddenly, he got scared.

Do I have PTSD? Is my dad giving it to me? Would I treat someone the way he treats me?

Tyler's first thought was of Sara. He couldn't imagine himself ever hurting her.

But what if he did? Not on purpose, but on accident.

Then it felt like his whole body was shaking.

He felt some tears fall. He felt empty. He felt vulnerable. His tough façade was a joke.

Tyler wanted to give in to the pain. He wanted to break down and sob.

But he didn't. Or he couldn't.

Breathe, he told himself. *Breathe.*

Tyler clenched his fist. He was trying to tighten his whole body.

Tyler knew eventually that this feeling would pass. It had to.

Tyler Ruiz had work to do.

Chapter 46

SHOW #2

Tyler and Sara continued hanging out on breaks and during lunch. They also hung out after school. He was conscientious and tried to give her space.

He felt weird playing it cool. Usually after scoring with a girl, the hot romance tapered off. He would get bored and move on to a new conquest.

Tyler didn't want to move on. Part of him wondered if he eventually would. He told himself not to think about it. So far, the more time he spent with Sara, the more time he wanted to spend with her. She seemed to like him too.

They stood outside the Observatory that Saturday night making out. Tyler was stoked. In his mind this was their way of declaring what they meant to each other in a public way.

Inside, the club was packed. There were many people still trying to get in. The headlining band was 7 Seconds. Playing before them were the Adolescents. The opening band was 411.

Had he been alone, Tyler would've wondered how he was going to get in. He figured if Sara wasn't worried about it, he wasn't going to say anything.

After a long period of locking lips, Sara hugged him. She pressed the side of her face into his chest. They didn't say anything. This moment made Tyler feel invincible.

She's letting me in, he told himself. *She trusts me. Even better, she needs me.*

Tyler wanted to be there for his dad. Even with all the awful things he'd done, Tyler still loved his father. Tyler was sure his father was deeply damaged. The war in Afghanistan had made him that way.

But Tyler's dad had never shown him the warmth that Sara was showing him right then. Not even when he was a kid. Not that Tyler could remember.

Tyler looked around. He saw Balchack, Hartsfield, and Doc. They were talking and smoking cigarettes. Standing next to them was Leslie.

She was looking right at Tyler. Tyler could tell by the way she stared at him that she wasn't mad. She was jealous. He gave her a sheepish smile.

"I see Leslie," Tyler said.

Sara shrugged and hugged Tyler harder.

"I don't think she's too happy with me right now," Tyler said.

"She's weird," Sara replied.

Later that night during the song "Creatures" by the Adolescents, Balchack and Hartsfield got Tyler into the pit. This time, Tyler knew what he was doing.

He moved to the music with lots of energy. Tyler made sure not to swing his arms. He bumped into people, but that was to be expected. The crowd sang along each time the singer held out the mic. Tyler tried to sing along too.

He took a break but didn't leave the pit. Tyler just moved off to the side. People there continued to sing. They also had the job of catching people who jumped off the stage. Other times, they had to help people float over the crowd.

During a break in one of the songs, the band was talking to the crowd. Tyler looked around and saw that Sara was in the balcony area.

She was talking to a big guy in a cut-off black T-shirt. He had a bunch of tattoos. What was left of this dude's hair was gray. He was obviously much older than Sara. He seemed older than everybody in the club.

The guy smiled slightly as he talked with her. Sara, on

the other hand, was talking a mile a minute. She was animated. It was almost like she was in awe of whoever this man was. She was almost hyper, like she had to keep this person's interest.

The Adolescents launched into their song "I Hate Children." The crowd went nuts again.

Chapter 47

CHASE

†yler and Sara had misjudged the bus schedule. Taking the bus had been her idea. She said she liked riding it.

"It adds a little bit of adventure to our travels," she'd told Tyler.

As a result, they had to walk home. The plan was they would get to her house and get her parents' car. Balchack and the others had left the show early. Apparently, there was a late-night show in the Inland Empire.

Tyler would've been up to going. Sara didn't want to. She said she was tired. Tyler knew that wasn't true. Leslie would probably be there. Sara just didn't want to deal with the possible drama.

They walked past an industrial area about a half-mile from the Observatory.

"Who was that old guy you were talking to?" Tyler asked, smiling. He didn't want Sara to think he was dissing her friend.

"My dad." Sara laughed.

"Come on."

"Are you jealous?" Sara smiled.

"No way. I'm totally hotter than that dude." They both laughed after Tyler said that.

"His name is Lisk. He's been around forever. He saw Minor Threat play. He's also seen every version of Black Flag. There's a rumor that he's one of the punks on the cover of the Circle Jerks 'Group Sex' album."

"Oh." Tyler hadn't expected to get so much information. "I've just never seen you talk to anybody in that way."

"What way?" Sara eyed him sternly.

Tyler didn't want to pick a fight. He just wanted to know who the guy was. Sara wanted to be free, though. Tyler needed to remember that.

"Like you're impressed with them," Tyler said softly. He wanted Sara to take it as a compliment.

At that point, a car full of people drove by them.

"Buy some real clothes!" one of the people in the car yelled.

Sara stepped out into the street.

"My hot boyfriend's gonna kick your ass!" Sara yelled.

Tyler laughed. He was stoked that Sara had called him her boyfriend. But before he could let the words sink in, Tyler felt his stomach tighten.

It wasn't because of Sara. She smiled as she walked over to him.

He was staring at the car. It had stopped and was backing up.

Chapter 48

WILD IN
THE STREETS

Run," Tyler said, taking her hand.

They ran off into the industrial area. Tyler's hope was they could become invisible amid all the identical white buildings.

The car came after them.

Tyler wasn't sure how far in they went. Then he turned, still holding Sara's hand, and took her back down another row of buildings. If there was a confrontation, Tyler didn't want to be trapped inside the complex.

Tyler noticed that Sara was laughing the whole time. It was the same wild-eyed laugh she had given him in the park. It looked like she had fire in her eyes.

They came to a small group of buildings toward the

front. There was a slight opening between them. Tyler felt they were safe there. Safe enough to catch their breath.

"We should be okay here for a while." Tyler continued to look around.

Sara grabbed him and started kissing him. It was fast, passionate, and like nothing else Tyler had ever experienced. He fell back against a wall. Tyler tried to steady himself, but Sara was relentless.

Tyler held her in his arms. Sara kissed him ferociously. He pivoted and pinned her against the wall. But he knew he needed to keep his guard up. With the people who were chasing them. And with Sara, who was too wrapped up in trying to seduce him.

He'd never felt more alive.

PLANS

As Tyler turned to go to biology, he was met with a big hug and kiss from Sara. She wrapped her arms tightly around his neck. She kissed him with the same passion she had kissed him on Saturday night.

She wore a short black skirt, fishnet stockings, blue Doc Marten boots, and a loose-fitting shirt that read DK for Dead Kennedys on it.

"Let's do something after school," he said as he took her hand.

"Sure. You wanna go to the mall?" She eyed all the students as they walked together.

"Whatever."

They passed Adam, who shouldered Tyler. It was no accident. Adam was with Anthony.

Tyler and Adam stared at one another. Then Adam looked at Sara.

"What's up, girl?" Adam grinned.

"Hey, Adam." Sara smiled.

Tyler could tell they knew each other. Maybe they had even been friends at one point. Just the thought made Tyler want to hit Adam again.

"Don't even," Tyler said.

"Don't even what?" Adam shouted back.

They moved toward each other. Suddenly, Leon appeared out of nowhere.

"Adam?" Leon eyed Tyler. "Tyler? We have a problem here?"

"Not on my end," Adam said. "Everything's gonna be just fine. Bye, Sara."

Adam held her in his gaze. Sara laughed to herself and shook her head. Adam disappeared into the crowd, and Leon walked away.

Tyler was seething. He hated that Adam knew Sara. He hated that she seemed to know him. Even worse, he hated that they both knew he hated it. Tyler already felt vulnerable enough.

Why can't I just have something in my life that's easy? he asked himself.

Sara pulled at his hand as he stubbornly followed her.

"I hate that guy," he said.

"He's not my favorite either." Sara smiled at Tyler.

"I shoulda hit him again."

"Whoa!" Sara's tone was exaggerated. "Down, boy!"

"How do you two even know each other?"

"Am I that much of an outcast?" Sara was serious now. She had a way of doing that to Tyler. Luring him in with one emotion, and then turning it around on him. "I can't know the hot quarterback?"

"Why would you want to know him?" Tyler asked.

"I don't want to know him." Sara smiled again. "We were partners last year in drama class."

Sara could see that explanation wasn't cutting it.

"You guys have a kissing scene?"

"No." Sara looked away. "And don't worry, you're much better than he is."

Tyler froze. He hated how mad this was making him. How mad she was making him. And she wasn't even trying to. Not really.

"If you really know the difference between us," he said slowly, "that's gross."

"I don't." Sara could tell she'd hurt Tyler. She hugged him and kissed his cheek. "Somebody's sensitive today."

"I just hate everything about that guy. I'm sorry." Tyler eyed Sara.

She looked at him. Sara wasn't smiling anymore. They kissed again.

STORY IN PRINT

It hadn't taken Tyler nearly as long as he'd thought it would to type up "Skinhead Chick." It came out of the printer at Mr. Zamora's desk. The teacher was listening to the band Fugazi, eating his lunch, and grading papers.

"I hope she likes this story," Tyler said. He was too excited to eat the free lunch the school provided him.

"What girl wouldn't like being a superhero in their own story?" Mr. Zamora looked up at Tyler. He dropped another graded paper on his desk.

"I just …" Tyler didn't quite know how to say what he wanted to say. "I've never felt like this about anybody. Sara's so great. She's so special. She can do anything she wants. She does anything she wants. I just want her to know that I know."

"You made her a superhero." Mr. Zamora's tone was

very matter-of-fact. Tyler could tell he got what he was saying.

"She inspires me." Hearing himself say those words made Tyler feel weird. He liked Mr. Zamora, but he didn't know him very well. Tyler wasn't used to being open with his feelings.

"Hold on to that." Mr. Zamora stared at Tyler with a very serious expression. "That's one of the best things you can ever feel."

Tyler nodded his head.

"So your dad doesn't know how good a writer his son is?"

Tyler shrugged and looked back at the printer.

"He would if he could." Tyler had to tell himself this. He had to believe it. "He's messed up."

"Things ever get tense between you guys?"

"What do you think?" Tyler shot Mr. Zamora a look. He wasn't trying to be hard, but if Mr. Zamora wanted answers, he was going to get them.

"Let me know if it ever gets to be too much." Mr. Zamora looked at Tyler with concern.

Tyler appreciated that.

Chapter 51

No-Show

Tyler waited for Sara at their usual meeting spot where he had first seen her. He was holding the "Skinhead Chick" story and trying not to bend it.

Students were filing past him. They were talking, texting, and telling jokes. For the first time in a long time, Tyler didn't feel so far from being normal. He had Sara. They were going to walk out of school together. They had plans. Tyler had someone.

Eventually, all the students were gone. Tyler stood alone. Club members, the school band, and sports teams were the only ones left on campus.

Tyler watched the football team practice. He normally saw Adam on the field. He didn't see him today.

Why are you looking for him anyway? Tyler asked himself.

Realizing it had been almost an hour since school had gotten out, Tyler decided he was going to walk to Sara's house.

He knocked on the big wooden entrance door. It felt solid. Not über-cheap like the door of his apartment.

The door opened.

Tyler was expecting Sara. He figured she'd probably forgotten their plans.

It was her father.

"Hello?" Mr. Allen smiled.

"Uh, hi." Tyler could feel his heart starting to pound. "Is Sara home?"

"No, she's not. Are you a friend?" he asked politely.

What Tyler wanted to say was, "I'm her boyfriend."

"I'm Tyler." He paused. Sara's father's expression didn't change. He didn't know who Tyler was. Sara had never mentioned him. "I'm a friend from school. We were supposed to hang out today."

"Great." Her father stood back in the doorway. "As I said, she isn't home. You're more than welcome to wait for her inside."

He was inviting Tyler in with a broad sweep of his hand.

"Thanks." Tyler smiled and walked inside.

too Close to the Flame

Oh, they're a great band," Sara's dad said. They were talking about Led Zeppelin.

"I love Black Dog," Tyler offered.

"I remember when I first heard that," Sara's dad said. He took a sip of his water. He had offered Tyler something to drink, but Tyler wasn't thirsty. "My mom played it for me after she bought the cassette at a swap meet."

They both laughed. Tyler's dad used to have cassettes.

He looked around Sara's large house. There were pictures on the wall, nice furniture, and area rugs on the hardwood floors. To Tyler, this place was a palace.

"You ever listen to Motorhead?" Sara's dad asked.

"A little. 'Ace of Spades,'" Tyler stated. "Everybody knows that song."

"I almost collected all their stuff on cassette. Of course, this was back in the eighties. They've done a lot more since then."

Tyler couldn't believe how cool Sara's dad was. He was nothing like how she described him.

The door to the house opened. Sara walked in.

She stared at Tyler awkwardly.

"Sara," her dad said. "Come join us. Tyler and I were just talking about music."

"Okay," she said slowly.

She stared at the ground for a moment. It was just like Tyler had seen her do in OCS the first time. He could tell something was wrong.

"Can I talk to you outside, Tyler?"

"Sure," he said. "Great talking with you, Mister Allen."

"You too." Sara's dad extended his hand. "Sara always keeps her friends from her mother and me."

They shook hands, and Tyler followed Sara out of the house.

Chapter 53

NERVOUS BREAKDOWN

Tyler went over to Sara to give her a kiss. She turned around to face him and pushed him away.

"Hey," he said, taking out the "Skinhead Chick" story from his pocket. He had folded it up. "I wrote this for you."

Sara took the story and proceeded to rip it up. Tyler watched as his work littered the walkway of Sara's expensive home.

"I don't want anything from a double agent!" she yelled.

"What are you talking about?"

"Why are you here? Are you spying on me? Why are you invading my life?" She pushed him.

"We had plans." He held up his hands to stop her from pushing him again. "You didn't show. I came over. Your dad let me in. That's it!"

"I'll bet that's what happened!" Sara hissed.

"It is!" Tyler couldn't believe this. She was back to hating him again. "If anybody should be mad, it's me! You call me your boyfriend. Your parents don't even know I exist!"

"You're such a liar!" she screamed. "I can't believe I trusted you!"

"I'm the liar?!" Tyler yelled. Sara winced. "You talk about being open and free, but your the most closed-off person I've ever met."

"Yeah," she started, "I'm closed off from—"

"One day you're one way, the next day you're another. You want to be different, Sara, but you aren't. You're just like all the other punk posers who think they're *so* unique."

Sara's eyes got really big. Before he knew what was happening, she rushed him.

She scratched Tyler's throat, his face, whatever she could get her hands on. Tyler tried to grab her, but she was too fast. He finally grabbed one hand. That's when she slapped him.

As they made eye contact, Sara kicked him in the leg. Tyler figured it was her way of saying she wasn't sorry.

He finally got both hands. Tyler pulled her toward him. He held her against his chest. She started kicking his legs and stepping on his feet. She even tried to bite his hands.

"Listen, Sara," Tyler said calmly and softly. He didn't

care what she tried to do to him. He just wanted to hurt her with his words. "Birdy, you can call yourself a skinhead, a punker, or whatever … you're just crazy. I don't need this or you."

He pushed her away from him and walked away.

Tyler was worried she would come after him again. Then he heard her harsh, wailing sobs. Sara was bawling now. She was fighting to get air in her lungs as she cried.

As bad as this made Tyler feel, there was no way he was going back to see if she was okay.

Chapter 54

DISTANCE

Tyler didn't speak to Sara for the next week in school. He half-heartedly looked around for her, but she never appeared. He wasn't too sure he wanted to speak to her.

There was something about what they had. What they experienced. Tyler didn't want to let that go. He knew he was being foolish. The fact was he really cared about her despite everything that had happened.

Tyler finally called her. He used the phone in his apartment. His dad was sleeping in his bedroom. Tyler wanted to call when he wasn't home, but his dad always seemed to be home.

"This is Sara," her voice mail said. "Leave a message. If I like you, I'll call you back. If I don't like you, then piss off."

Tyler smiled after he heard that. That was Sara. That

was who he was attracted to. Not that girl on the front lawn of her parents' house.

Still, Tyler knew she was part of the deal. The other Sara. He couldn't just have one part of her. Tyler had to be all in.

"Hey, Sara. It's Tyler. I'm sorry about what I said a week ago. I really care about you. Please call me back."

Tyler put the phone down. That's when he heard his dad behind him. Tyler had been so focused on the phone call, he'd tuned everything out. He hadn't heard his dad come into the room.

"Listen up, Tyler." His dad's tone was low, but Tyler could hear it dripping with disdain. "Your mom may have died, but when she was alive, she treated me with respect."

Tyler didn't know what possessed him. He turned around and glared at his dad. They were eye to eye, inches from each other.

"I wouldn't have let it be any other way!" his dad screamed.

Instinctively, Tyler clenched his fists. At that moment, he wanted nothing more than to bash his dad's face in. Tyler knew it would have felt good.

Just like it did with Adam. Just like with all those other people he'd hit.

Again, Tyler managed to control himself. He turned and walked out of the apartment.

Chapter 55

OUTLET

After a few more days of not talking, seeing, or hearing anything from Sara, Tyler was desperate. He did a sweep of the campus.

When he didn't find her, he went to Mr. Zamora's classroom. The door was locked.

He has a teacher conference, Tyler reminded himself.

Tyler sat down at a planter in one of the secluded areas on campus. He took out his journal.

His stomach turned a bit as he flipped past the "Skinhead Chick" story. He couldn't even bother to look at the words he'd written.

She didn't even read it, he thought.

He was getting really depressed and sad.

Maybe Sara left the school, he wondered. *Her parents*

are papered up. They could send her anywhere she wanted to go.

Tyler couldn't believe that Sara would leave Banks High School because of him.

She's too tough and strong. She wouldn't go anywhere unless she really wanted to go there.

Tyler also refused to believe that she really hated him.

He found a blank page and started writing about Sara.

This wasn't a superhero story. Tyler just wrote about her. About everything she meant to him. All the emotions she evoked.

The words poured out onto the page. Tyler couldn't stop describing her.

There aren't enough words to say this right, he kept thinking. Still, he kept writing.

And as he did, Tyler realized why this fire for Sara burned so strong. Even after all that had happened.

He was in love with her. Tyler didn't care what had happened at her house. He didn't care what was wrong with her.

Even if she's crazy, like Balchack said.

Tyler just wanted to be there for Sara.

Unconditionally.

He wanted another chance. He didn't care that he didn't understand why she'd gotten so upset.

It was all part of why he loved Sara so much.

As he wrote, he became resolute.

I have to make it work between us, he told himself.

Tyler was so into what he was writing, he didn't notice Adam, Anthony, and Donovan surrounding him.

Bootboy Beatdown

I guess what Sara really wanted was to be with someone on the team." Adam's words completely removed Tyler from his thoughts.

He glared up at him.

"What?" Tyler stared at Adam and his friends. He knew he should probably stand up. He was in the wrong fighting position if he had to take on all of these guys.

"Your girl." Adam laughed. "That crazy punk chick. She was all over me last night, bro."

Tyler sprang to his feet. He was inches from Adam's face now. The only thing holding him back were Anthony and Donovan.

"She works fast, man," Adam continued. "I barely got out of our sesh with everything intact."

"You're such a liar!" Tyler didn't think he could hate

anybody more than he hated his dad. At that moment, Adam had his father beat by miles.

Tyler tried to break away from Anthony and Donovan. He used every ounce of energy he had. But they were too strong.

Adam pulled out his iPhone.

Tyler couldn't believe what he was showing him.

It was Adam and Sara. Together. They were both naked. Adam flipped though the photos without emotion. He stopped on one of him and Sara making out.

Tyler looked away. It was too much. He found himself getting angrier. Everything was slowly going black. Just like it always did. Only Tyler couldn't do anything about it.

"Don't worry, bro." Adam put another naked picture of Sara in Tyler's face. "I only Snapchatted that one. Good thing those pictures go away, right?"

Anthony and Donovan threw Tyler to the ground. It didn't hurt. Then they started kicking him. But that didn't hurt either.

Somehow, Tyler grabbed one of their legs. He twisted it at the ankle as hard as he could.

"Ahhh!" Donovan screamed as he fell to the ground.

These guys had no idea how tough Tyler was. No. Idea.

As the punches and kicks continued, Tyler moved through them. The hits had no effect on him. Eventually, he was on his feet.

Tyler slugged Anthony in the face. He flew backward and fell over the planter Tyler had been sitting at only moments before.

Adam started to run, but Tyler jumped on him. They fell to the ground. Tyler hit him on the back of his head. He did it as hard as he could.

Adam was screaming for Tyler to stop. Tyler couldn't hear him. He was going to kill him.

"Hey!" a voice called.

In the distance, Tyler saw Leon and another muscular member of campus security. They were coming over on a golf cart.

Somehow, Tyler composed himself. He grabbed his backpack and his journal.

He took off across the football field. Tyler found an opening in the fence. He squeezed through.

Campus security was still after him. They would probably call the cops.

Tyler didn't care. He would be long gone before they got there.

Chapter 57

†RUE LOVE

†yler ran to Sara's house. He knocked on the door.

No answer.

Tyler knocked a few more times. Then he tried the knob. To his surprise, the door was unlocked.

Tyler walked into the hallway. He was nervous. He had no idea what Sara's frame of mind was.

What if she's still mad? he asked himself. *What if she attacks me again?*

Tyler's first thought: he hoped she would. He was mad too. He wanted to show her she couldn't play him like this. She had betrayed him by hooking up with Adam.

Then he heard a noise. It was low. It sounded like a cat. Tyler didn't think Sara had one. She'd never mentioned it before.

Tyler followed the noise. It led him upstairs.

As Tyler got closer to Sara's bedroom, he realized what the noise was.

It was Sara. She was crying.

Tyler took a deep breath. He slowly pushed the door to the room open.

It squeaked as it opened, revealing her. Sara was curled up in a ball on the bed. She was wearing a sweatshirt and some navy blue pajama bottoms.

She had shaved her head completely. She had a thick head of stubble. It was patchy, so Tyler figured she did it herself.

Sara, sobbing, looked at him.

Any anger he had about her getting mad at him and hooking up with Adam was gone.

For a moment, Tyler thought Sara was just trying to hurt him. Then he realized the gravity of the mental illness she was dealing with. Sara was the way she was because she couldn't be any other way.

Tyler realized he didn't care about what Sara had done. He realized that his feelings for her were stronger than anything that might come between them.

"I wanna help you, Sara." Tyler tried to smile.

"I'm sorry," she said softly. Her voice sounded raspy.

Tyler slowly lay down on the bed next to her. He put his arm on hers. Tyler rested his head on the pillow.

"You don't have to be sorry for anything, Sara. I love

you." As soon as Tyler heard himself say the words to her, he felt better. "Whether we're together or not, I love you."

"He raped me," Sara cried. "I was mad and I led him on, but then he wouldn't stop. I told him to stop. I begged him to stop but he wouldn't."

Tyler pressed his hand against her shoulder.

"Shhh, you have nothing to be sorry for. None of this is your fault."

He kissed her shaved head.

Sara continued talking and crying.

Tyler just lay next to her. Listening.

Chapter 58

CHOICES

As Tyler walked home, he ran through the everything in his mind.

Consoling Sara. Holding her and talking with her for hours.

I'd do it all again right now if she asked me to.

Tyler wanted to call the police. It wasn't just because he hated Adam.

He didn't know how many other girls he'd done this to.

"It doesn't matter if it's your word against his," Tyler told Sara. "You said no. You told him to stop. Rape is rape."

"Nobody will care," she'd protested through tears.

"They will."

"They won't! Nobody cares about me!" Sara's voice was rising.

Tyler stopped talking about it with her. He knew Sara needed time. She needed to work this out. He was going to help her.

Tyler told her he was going to do whatever was needed to make her okay.

"I'll never be okay," Sara said as she wiped away more tears. "I've never been."

Chapter 59

Not taking It Anymore

You been fighting again?!" Tyler's dad's voice barked the minute he walked into his apartment.

Tyler didn't put his backpack down. He knew he wouldn't be staying long.

Slap!

Tyler's father's hand bounced off his head. He wasn't surprised. Tyler knew this was coming.

"Don't do that again." Tyler eyed his dad coldly. "I'm warning you."

"You got in another fight? You think you're tough? Fight me!"

Again his dad's hand came down. Tyler grabbed his dad by the shirt collar. He shook him. Tyler had to use all of his strength. His dad had lost some muscle over the years, but he was still plenty strong.

Tyler slammed him into the wall. A cheesy landscape picture fell to the floor. The frame broke into pieces.

He took his father and threw him on the couch. Tyler didn't want to hurt him. He didn't want his dad to call the cops and get Tyler in trouble either.

"That the best you got?" His dad sat up. He had a gash on his cheek.

"All you want to do is hurt me!" Tyler yelled. "I can't take it anymore! I'm sorry about the war—"

"Don't talk about that!" His dad's voice was much louder than Tyler's. "You don't know anything about it!"

"I'm sorry about what happened over there." Tyler had tears in his eyes. He couldn't help it.

"Shut up! I'm warning you." His dad raised his hand again.

"What do you think you're doing to me?!" Tyler screamed. "I'm your son! And you hate me! Well, you know what, Dad? I hate you too."

Tyler's dad grabbed for him. Tyler stepped back and his father fell to the floor.

They stared at one another.

Tyler's dad sat back against the couch. He was breathing so heavily it sounded like he was hyperventilating.

"Dad? Are you okay?" Tyler moved toward him.

"We were going down the road." His father's voice cracked a bit. Tyler didn't know what was happening. "Like we always did. The same road. We saw the same people we always did."

His dad's voice started to shake. Tyler saw tears well up in his father's eyes. He couldn't believe what he was witnessing. His father was breaking down.

"We made plans for that night. Smith was leaving the next morning. Going back home to the States. We were gonna barbecue. To celebrate."

"Dad …" Tyler wanted to let his dad know he didn't need to do this to himself. He didn't need to do this to them.

"This little girl … on the side of the road. She smiled at me. Like always …" Tears were streaming down his father's cheeks now. "Then … the ground just opened it. It was so loud. We all turned over. There were pieces of the Humvee everywhere. All of my friends were everywhere. I grabbed my gun. I was shooting at anything I could. I had to find that girl. I had to kill …"

Tyler's dad was shaking now. Tyler moved over to him. He put his hand out.

His father whacked it away. It didn't hurt. For some reason, it surprised Tyler.

"Don't you move! I'll kill all of you! Don't you move!" his father shrieked.

Tyler backed up slowly. He didn't say another word. He didn't even breathe. Tyler grabbed his backpack, opened the door, and let himself out of the apartment.

Tyler's dad continued yelling at whoever or whatever was in his head.

LESSER OF TWO EVILS

Tyler stopped walking and stood under a streetlight. It was about a half-mile from his apartment. As he looked around, he figured that it was probably close to nine o'clock. There were people walking around. Cars on the road.

Some of the people looked like they lived on the streets. Their clothes didn't fit right. They were dirty. Some of them talked to themselves.

Tyler shook his head as he looked around.

I can't leave him, he told himself. *I have nowhere to go.*

He walked back to Via Joaquin. He went to the tables. His writing sanctuary. Tyler sat down. He put his backpack on the bench next to him.

Tyler clenched his fists. He gritted his teeth. And then he started to cry. He buried his face in his hands and just cried.

He cried for his mother.

His father.

He cried for Sara.

He wished he could cry for himself.

Eventually, Tyler fell asleep.

Tyler woke up to the rising sun. Neighbors were starting to get ready for the day. Doors were opening and closing. Babies were crying. Parents were telling their kids what they wanted them to do.

He rested his head in his arms for a moment. Then he got up and went to his apartment.

Tyler slowly opened the door. His dad was in his bedroom. Tyler was relieved to hear the familiar sounds of snoring. Tyler hoped his dad had found some peace when he slept.

He walked over to the cabinet and took out a granola bar. His dad had picked them up at the dollar store. Tyler wanted to shower, but it was almost seven o'clock. He had to get to school.

Chapter 61

BOMBSHELL

Tyler walked into the Banks High School discipline department.

"I was fighting yesterday," he told the lady who was in charge of calling campus security. "I bailed fifth and sixth period. Sorry."

The woman behind the desk didn't seem to know what to do. Students probably didn't turn themselves in too often.

After consulting with Vice Principal Ward, Tyler was placed in OCS. He didn't know how long he was going to be there this time, but he figured it would be a while. Later he was taken into the gym where all the sophomores were. They were sitting at tables.

He found out that today was a half-day. The school was administering a state test. Today they were doing the

English portion. Before Tyler knew what was happening, he was reading paragraphs and answering multiple-choice questions.

"I thought this was all on computer now?" he heard one student say.

Tyler didn't care. He was just happy to be back in school. At least he knew the rules there.

During breaks in testing, Tyler spent his time writing about Sara. He was going to reprint the "Skinhead Chick" story and give it to her. He also wanted to give her the new piece he was writing.

When school got out at noon, he made his way over to Sara's house. Realizing he hadn't eaten anything since the granola bar, Tyler suddenly felt very hungry. He thought about eating at Sara's house, but he didn't want to do that. Not if her parents were home. Tyler felt like he would be imposing too much.

He had a couple of dollars on him. It was all that was left of the fifteen from a few weeks before. He went into a small burger place called DGBs.

He got a large order of french fries. It was all he could afford. It would also fill him up best.

"Tyler?" he heard a voice say as he picked up his order. Tyler turned around and saw Leslie standing behind him.

Sara's girlfriend Leslie.

She wore her hair pulled back. She had on a shirt that read D.I. across the chest. Leslie wore black jeans and Chuck Taylors, just like Sara.

"Hey," he said. "What's up?"

"I know I don't know you, but have you seen Sara recently?"

If Leslie were a guy, Tyler thought they might fight. He didn't know how things worked with girls.

"Yesterday. I went to her house."

"Oh …"

"Why?"

"Well." Leslie took a deep breath. "She called this guy Lisk that we know. She called him last night."

"I've heard of him."

"She asked if he could get her a pipe bomb. He told her no. And apparently she flipped out on him. I tried to get in touch with her yesterday and today, but she's not answering her phone. She does that. If she gets really upset with someone, she'll turn off her phone. That way she won't have to talk to anybody."

They stared at each other. The wheels turned in Tyler's head. The first image he saw was one of the pictures of Sara and Adam.

"Why do you think she'd want a bomb?" Leslie asked.

Tyler ran out of the restaurant without answering.

Chapter 62

FRANTIC

†yler entered Banks High School.

Adam's locker, he told himself.

On the way there, he spotted a paperclip on the ground. Tyler picked it up and unfolded one part of it.

Tyler had seen Adam at his locker a few times. He didn't know the number, but it was the last one in its row. It was right next to the glass door of the math building.

He stared at it. The locker didn't look different than any of the others. Tyler put his hand on it and rattled it back and forth a few times.

It seemed fine.

Tyler put the open end of the paperclip into the lock. He didn't even look around to see if anybody was looking. He couldn't. Tyler didn't know how much time he had.

He jiggled the paperclip. He heard a few clicks. A few

times Tyler thought he had cracked the code. He tried opening the door but nothing happened.

After a few more clicks with nothing happening, Tyler eventually got the locker open.

As the door swung open, Tyler took a deep breath. If it had a bomb inside, it might blow up. Tyler would probably be dead. And anyone else unlucky enough to be close.

He moved the door back and forth slightly. Nothing happened.

All that was inside the locker were Adam's books and a picture of him and Cassie.

Tyler heard a whistle blow. He heard cheers from the cheerleaders.

"Football lockers," he said out loud.

Tyler took off toward the football field. The place he never wanted to go again. Now he was going there to possibly save the life of somebody he hated.

Chapter 63

So Far Away

Tyler pushed his way into the locker room.

"Hey!" someone yelled.

"Why's he back here?" another player asked.

Tyler couldn't think about them.

He spotted Adam and Anthony making their way toward their lockers. They both had visible bruises on their faces from where Tyler had punched them. When they stopped walking, Tyler knew where their lockers were.

"Adam!" he yelled.

The locker room was too loud. They didn't hear him.

Tyler saw Adam looking at his locker.

He's doing the combo! Tyler told himself.

"Adam!" Tyler called again. "Stop!"

Adam looked up. Tyler ran to him. He was so quick nobody had a chance to get between them.

"Don't open it!" Tyler blocked the locker.

"Dude! You must have a death wish." Adam pushed him, but Tyler wouldn't budge.

All of Adam's friends started to grab him. Anthony even hit Tyler on the side of the head.

"I'm trying to help you," Tyler stared hard into Adam's eyes.

"Why are you here?" Coach Galloway asked. He walked up with Assistant Coach Wagner behind him.

"Call the bomb squad," Tyler said to Coach Galloway.

"What are you talking about?"

"He's lying, Coach. He's just messing with me. He's crazy like his psycho girlfriend." Adam grabbed for his lock, but Tyler moved in front of it.

"You need to clear the room," Tyler practically begged.

He had to stop Adam. He had to help this situation. Tyler had to make things okay for Sara.

"I'm not letting you open my locker!"

"It's probably not set up right. Wouldn't know how … Just angry because …" Tyler stopped talking. He didn't want to say anything to endanger Sara and get Adam even more pissed.

Adam had raped her. And Tyler was going to see that it got handled, but right now he had to think about the pipe bomb and not blowing up the school.

"I'll open it." Adam shoved Tyler out of the way. He

started doing his combination. Most of Adam's friends let go of Tyler.

Adam pulled the lock off.

"Hey! Don't do that. Careful now," Coach Galloway ordered. He looked back at the team. "Out of the locker room! Clear this place! Everybody out!"

It took a few minutes, but everybody eventually cleared out.

"Let's wait for the bomb squad, Adam," Coach Galloway said.

Tyler couldn't wait. He pulled open the locker door.

"Wait—" Coach Galloway started to say.

Sitting in the middle of the locker on top of Adam's clothes was a metal tube. The wires had apparently been connected to the door. They must've got disconnected when Tyler opened it. It looked fake. And harmless.

"You were right," Adam said. "That crazy bitch was too stupid to set it up right."

Tyler headed out of the locker room.

He heard Adam calling for him.

He heard Coach Galloway calling for him.

He even heard them yelling for other people to stop him. All the players looked at Tyler as he bolted.

Chapter 64

Do or Die

Tyler made his way over to Sara's house. Then he stopped.

Where would she be? he asked himself. Tyler knew she wasn't home.

Sara didn't feel safe there. That house didn't mean anything to her. It was just somewhere to sleep. Where would Sara go?

Then it hit Tyler. He started running in the opposite direction. Toward the Observatory.

Without people inside, the Observatory seemed small. It wasn't as intimidating either. At first, Soto wasn't going to let Tyler in.

"I'm Sara's boyfriend," Tyler insisted. "Please."

Soto stared at Tyler for a moment. Then he moved out of the way.

As Tyler stood in the empty area where the bands

played, he heard a sound. It was the whimpering he had heard when he found Sara at her house the day before.

She's here, he told himself.

"Sara!" Tyler called.

No response.

He followed the sound of the whimpering. It led to the balcony. Tyler made his way up there. That's where he found her.

Sara sat against the wall in the darkest corner. She was in the same clothes she had been in the day before. Her head was down. She was resting it in her arms. She looked like a Minor Threat album cover she had shown him.

She also had a gun.

Tyler didn't know what kind it was. He just knew he had to choose his words carefully and let Sara know he was her friend above all else.

"Sara," Tyler said softly. "I'm here to help you."

She didn't say anything. She continued sobbing.

"Can I have the gun? Please?"

"No." Sara still didn't look at him.

"Who gave it to you?"

"Dominic. He's friends with Lisk. I hate Lisk now. He wouldn't help me. He's a traitor."

"I want you to know everything is going to be okay." Tyler moved closer. "Adam didn't open his locker. I stopped him. The bomb didn't go off."

"You what?!" Sara looked Tyler. The dim overhead lights of the Observatory showed her face. It was puffy and swollen from crying. "You're just like all the rest. You double-crossed me. Just like everybody else!"

"I'm not. Would I be here if I was like everybody else? I just want you to be okay."

"I'll never be okay!" she yelled. Her voice echoed throughout the club. "Just let me end it, Tyler. Nobody will care anyway."

Sara started to lift the gun. Tyler reached over and blocked her. He tried to be as gentle as possible. He was afraid it might accidentally go off.

"You don't need to keep hurting yourself, Sara. You just need to be you." Tyler felt himself starting to cry. He didn't care. He was going to do whatever it took to help her. "That's why I love you. That's why your parents love you. Everything's going to be okay. Just, please, let us help you."

"I don't need help! I don't need help!" Sara started to bawl.

She lifted the gun again. Tyler ripped it from her cold fingers and put it next to him.

Sara reached for it. Tyler grabbed her hands. Sara started to kick him. She began to hit him with her fists.

Tyler stood up. He put the gun in the back of his jeans.

Sara lunged for him. He stepped backward, and she seemed to splatter on the floor. Just like his father had. She let out a loud wail and began sobbing again. It was loud. Tyler had never heard anybody cry so hard.

Then she began to hit herself. She started clawing at her arms, her face, anywhere she could dig in her fingernails.

Tyler ran to put the gun on a small table in the balcony lobby. He sprinted back to Sara and got on the ground beside her. He wrapped himself around her. He grabbed her arms and hands.

Sara continued to cry and scream. She tried to scratch Tyler as well. He didn't care.

Tyler wasn't going to let go. He didn't care what happened to him. He wasn't going to let Sara hurt herself anymore.

After what seemed like forever, Sara calmed down. They lay on the ground. Entwined. Sara continued to breathe heavily.

"I used to think nobody cared about me too," Tyler whispered in her ear. "But when I realized how much I care about you … How much you mean to me … Sara, that made up for everything. I love you, no matter what."

Chapter 65

ALL IN

Tyler told Sara he was going to call her parents. She agreed by nodding her head. Soto let him use his cell phone. When he got the Allens on the phone, they were already upset. The police were there.

"Is it true?" they asked desperately. "Sara brought a bomb to school?"

"Yeah." Tyler didn't tell them about the gun she had.

Her parents got to the Observatory around the same time as the police. To Tyler's surprise, the police were really cool. They allowed Sara's mom to administer her medication before they talked to her.

Right before she sat down with them, Tyler noticed something. Sara had an expression he had never seen before.

Fear.

He took her hand in his and sat with her through the whole process. Sara told the police and her parents about the bomb, the gun, and Adam.

There were many times during the conversation when she got very emotional. It wasn't just crying. She'd start talking fast and have to take a breath. She would answer a question, then become defiant. Every emotion Sara had was on display. Until her medication kicked in.

The hardest part for Tyler was when she looked at him. Those confident eyes were now scared and unsure of what she should and shouldn't say.

LAST RESORT

Sara was sent home with her parents and a police escort. Tyler was surprised. He was sure they were going to arrest her and take her to juvenile detention.

"It's different for someone like her," Sara's dad told him. "She'll face justice. But she's mentally ill."

They gave Tyler a ride home.

"Thank you for everything," Sara's mom said. Her eyes were bloodshot from crying so much.

"Yeah, Tyler," her father said, shaking his hand. "We really appreciate you. You were there for our daughter."

"No problem." Tyler smiled.

He looked in the back at Sara. She was sleeping. She'd fallen asleep when they got in the car.

Sara was at peace. Tyler wanted to leave her that way.

Tyler didn't even notice all the people hanging around Via Joaquin. Normally, he kept his guard up. He didn't want any of them messing with him. He couldn't even think about them tonight.

The second he walked into his apartment, he heard his dad. He was snoring. The apartment was pitch black except for a small light in the kitchen. His dad liked it on so he could see if he got up.

The couch looked comfortable. Then Tyler thought better of it. It'd be just like his dad to wake up. He'd come out of his room and mess with Tyler.

Tyler didn't think he could take it tonight. He didn't know what he would do to his father if that happened.

He stepped out of the apartment and shut the door. Tyler went to his writing spot and put his head down. He could sleep there. He knew he could get at least five hours. Then he'd have to get up for school.

SKINHEAD GLORY

As Tyler approached Banks High School that morning, he realized he'd forgotten to eat breakfast. He had so much on his mind, there wasn't any room to think about eating. Usually, Tyler always felt like eating. But after all that had happened, he wasn't hungry anyway.

His heart raced when he saw two police cars out front.

I thought Sara and her family worked most of that out last night.

Were they looking into her background? Were they confiscating things she had used? Gathering evidence?

Then he saw Adam. He was being escorted by two police officers. He was in handcuffs.

As Tyler got closer, Adam saw him. He stared. He smirked at Tyler. Then he turned his head.

All of Adam's swagger disappeared. In an instant he was no longer the cool guy. The person Tyler hated and envied for having everything would no longer be a distraction. Adam was in a lot of trouble. Starting that morning, his life was never going to be the same.

Chapter 68

OPTIONS

This is a great story." Mr. Zamora smiled as he put it on his desk. It was piled high with more papers he needed to correct, but he'd taken time to read Tyler's story. "Did she like it?"

"She hasn't read it yet." Tyler knew that Mr. Zamora knew a lot about what had happened. He'd never asked Tyler anything straight out. And Tyler appreciated that.

"She's gonna love it." Mr. Zamora smiled. "You can really write, Tyler. I am insisting that next semester you take honors English."

"I'll think about it. As long as you're teaching it."

"I will be. Everything okay with you otherwise?"

Tyler knew he wasn't asking about Sara. He wanted to know about his dad.

"Yeah, things are okay," Tyler lied. "I just … I don't

understand. Why can I accept how Sara is but I can't accept that about my dad?"

"It's probably because she's your girlfriend. And he's your dad. Your expectations are different."

"I just want him to take care of me. Like a father should." Tyler hated hearing himself admit that. "I know that sounds dumb."

"You don't need to live like this, Tyler. If your dad can't do it … if things are too rough at home, there are places you can go to live."

"Where? The street? That's where he threatens to send me all the time." Tyler briefly felt himself get sad, then it passed.

"There are group homes. Other places." Tyler and Mr. Zamora made eye contact. "It may not be the best situation, but it's better than the one you're in. When you turn eighteen, you can go out on your own if you're able."

Tyler didn't want to think about it. Not now. He just wanted to enjoy being a sophomore if he could.

Maybe Sara and I will still be together then. We can get a place. That made Tyler feel better.

"Anything's possible. I think you can do anything you want." Mr. Zamora didn't smile after he said that.

He wanted Tyler to know he meant it.

Chapter 69

SETARI
REHAB FACILITY

Y ou go in first. She'll be happier to see you," Sara's dad said.

They were driving to the Setari Rehab Facility. As Sara was awaiting sentencing, this was deemed the best and safest place for her. Tyler figured that due to Sara's condition, she wouldn't go to juvenile hall. She'd just be in a place like Setari for a long time.

"Hopefully when she sees me, she'll be happy about it," Sara's dad continued. "She wasn't the last time I was here." Sara's dad eyed Tyler after he said that.

Tyler looked down at the copy of the "Skinhead Chick" story he was holding. He was trying not to wrinkle it, but it was getting wrinkled anyway.

"She'll be happy to see you," Tyler assured Sara's father. "She's just ... she's dealing with everything the best she can."

Tyler had spoken to her a couple of times from his apartment. He had called her at the specific times that patients could receive calls. Sara's parents had made sure Tyler knew what those were. It had been about five days since he had seen her, though. It felt like a lot longer than that.

The talks had been brief. Sara had cried a lot during the first one. She was quiet during the second. But she told Tyler she loved him both times.

"I hope she's dealing with things okay." Sara's dad eyed the Setari Rehab Facility as they drove up to it.

It didn't look like a medical facility at all. It looked more like a really nice apartment complex. Tyler imagined that Via Joaquin had looked like this many years ago.

"I love her so much, Tyler. I've just ... I've never been able to get close to her. I want to. I've tried, believe me I have."

"I think with Sara ..." Tyler was choosing his words carefully. Sara's dad was on the verge of tears. "You just have to keep trying."

"You're right." He smiled. "Man, Tyler. Sara's mom and I, we're so happy you're in her life."

Chapter 70

WHEN SHE BEGINS

Even after only five days, Sara's hair was a little longer. Since it was shaved, he could really see its natural brown color.

"Other than you and my parents," Sara started as they got situated on a bench, "the only person who has visited me was Leslie."

Tyler eyed the stone path that curved around some trees in the back of the mental health facility. The lawn was nicely cut and very green. Tyler thought it might be nice to write back there sometime.

"Balchack, Lisk, and everybody else probably hates me because of what I did. How I acted … the things I said to them. I went too far again. Like always."

Sara's voice cracked. Tyler put his arm around her. He could feel her starting to cry.

"Nobody hates you," he whispered. "They just want you to be okay."

"I think I've always cared too much about what people think of me. That's probably why I try so hard to act like I don't." Sara wiped her eyes.

"We all care too much about that. And we all say we don't." Tyler gave her a squeeze. "Your dad brought me here today. He wants to see you later. If that's okay."

Sara didn't respond.

"Leslie and I hooked up when she was here." Sara looked at Tyler. He kept staring at the grass and the trees. "It was nothing big. I just … as part of my recovery I want to be honest. I thought you should know."

"I just want you to be happy, Sara. That's all I really care about." He smiled.

Tyler was disappointed. He didn't understand why he couldn't be enough for Sara. Then he wondered if Leslie wondered the same thing about herself. Tyler knew he had to check these thoughts and feelings. Now was no time to be jealous or needy when Sara needed him most.

He looked at her. She looked down at the ground.

"Do you still want to be with me?" she asked quietly.

"Of course." Tyler nodded his head.

"You think you can handle being with the crazy girl?" Her voice sounded sassy like the Sara he had met a few months ago.

"Haven't I been with her this whole time?"

Tyler took the "Skinhead Chick" story out of his jacket. He was nervous at first. The last time he'd tried to give it to her didn't go so well.

"Here's that story I wrote for you. I can't wait for you to read it." Sara took it from Tyler and looked at it.

"'Skinhead Chick'?" Sara smiled. "Totally original title, Tyler."

"For an original girl."

He hoped she liked it. Tyler hoped it could help her in some way.

"You think I can be okay?" Sara looked up from the story.

Tyler looked at her. He looked deep into her eyes. Again, he saw an expression from Sara he had never seen before.

Vulnerability.

"Yes. I think you can be okay. I think you're gonna be okay," Tyler said quietly.

Sara took his hand in hers. They continued to look into each other's eyes. Slowly, Sara's expression returned to the confident one he had seen that first day she caught his eye. It was the one he couldn't stop thinking about.

The only difference was that this time Sara was looking right at him.

WANT to KEEP READING?

Turn the page for a sneak peek at another book from the Gravel Road series: L.B. Tillit's *Unchained*.

ISBN: 978-1-61651-792-2

CHAPTER 1

Bad

I wasn't born mean. I hated the word "mean." But being bad was great. It got Mom and Dad to at least look at me. And that's all I wanted.

I started being bad when I was little. Real little, like five. I couldn't figure out why Mom and Dad didn't play with me or touch me anymore. I remember that there had been times before when they did. I thought I had done something to make them stop. So I cried. When that didn't work, I would go up to them and hit. I was reaching for anything.

Mom and Dad didn't do much when I hit them. I wanted them to do something. Even hit me back. They just sat on the couch in a fog of smoke. The smoke made my head spin. I didn't get it then. I get it now. They were so high that they didn't know I was there.

It wasn't always bad with both of them. One time I

remember opening the fridge. I wanted something to eat. Anything. There were three things in the fridge. Milk, old cheese that looked green, and one can of soda. I couldn't open the soda, so I started to drink the milk. I put my lips on the jug and tried to drink it. Lumps filled my mouth. I choked a little. Then I spit out a sour mess all over my shirt and the floor. I screamed.

Dad walked in the kitchen. Standing in his boxers he looked at me and cursed. He looked at me. Actually looked at me. "TJ, you clean up that mess!" He threw me a towel, and I cried while I wiped the mess off of me and the floor.

Then I took the towel and threw it at his legs. The white lumps smeared his black legs like paint. I yelled, "I'm hungry!" I stood up and faced the man. "I hate you!" My little hands balled up in fists. I had pulled my shirt off, and I could see my stomach. Spots of white milk stuck to my own dark skin. I didn't care. I was mad. I was hungry.

Dad stared at for me a minute. Then he started to laugh. "Thomas Jahmal Young! You think you can take me?" He ran after me as I took off into the living room, if you could call it that. It had barely enough room for a small couch and TV. He tackled me in front of Mom. She was on the couch and woke up out of a deep sleep. She watched him pin me down. He was laughing. He took his nasty legs and wiped the curds all over my belly. I almost looked white. Then we both started laughing.

"What's going on?" Mom wasn't sure if she should get mad or not.

Dad held me for a moment longer. His grip loosened. I could feel something I hadn't felt in a long time. He rubbed my head and looked at Mom. "Baby, it looks like we need some food." He rubbed my skin. "Our milk has turned into paint."

I giggled. I hadn't giggled much lately.

Mom didn't smile. She turned over on the couch and said, "You go get some. Just leave me alone." Without looking at me she went back to sleep.

Here, Evan is recording a voice for his animated horror film, Insect.

About the Author

Evan Jacobs was born in Long Island, New York. His family moved to California when he was four years old. They settled in Fountain Valley, where he still lives today.

As a filmmaker, Evan has directed eleven low-budget films. He has also had various screenplays produced and realized by other directors. He co-wrote the film *Knock-out*, starring "Stone Cold" Steve Austin. He co-authored the thriller *Distant Shore.* He is currently juggling several movie and book projects.

Evan is also a behavior interventionist for people who have special needs. He works with a variety of students to make their days as successful as possible. His third young adult novel, *Screaming Quietly,* won a Moonbeam Children's Book Award bronze medal. You can find out more about him at www.anhedeniafilms.blogspot.com.